SISTERHOOD
OF THE
YELLOW ROSE

MYSTERY NOVELS by ALI ROBERTI

THE MEG RAVENHILL MYSTERIES

CAIRO

RUNNYMEDE

THE TESS RANKIN MYSTERIES

SISTERHOOD OF THE YELLOW ROSE

SISTERHOOD OF THE YELLOW ROSE

In memory of

DOROTHY GRACE BENNETT WHITE

WWII Army nurse, beloved mother and best friend

ACKNOWLEDGMENTS

I wish to acknowledge the assistance of the following people: my incredibly professional and speedy editor Renee Klemenok; my darling daughter Emma Roberti, the first person to read everything I write; my ever-faithful first readers, Maile Lilinoe, Patricia Atkinson, Laura Shooter, Julie Wesley, Tristan Atkinson and Chloe Spicher; Debbie Raby has patiently listened to me moan, groan and generally complain about the writing process for years, her wise refrain of, "Just keep writing," has kept me ambling along this often difficult path; my occupational therapist Tracey Airth-Edblom, OTD, OTR/L, CHT, in the middle of writing this novel I broke my arm and all of the bones in my wrist, without Tracey's months of therapy, encouragement and friendship, I would not have been able to finish this book; Captain Chuck Raby helped me with all of my nautical communication information; Alex Madias attempted to teach me the arcane world of computer programs, the Deep Web and cyber-security, only my readers can decide if I am an apt pupil; my interns Michael Bard, Mason Mize, and Edward Holt are an essential part of my life as a professor/writer; Matt Diack and Paul Cook, the proprietors of The Dairy Private Luxury hotel in Queenstown, New Zealand, took such good care of my family while I was researching this novel that I had to include their extraordinary hotel in my story; my son Bradley Roberti set up my author page on Facebook and generally handles all of my online presence; my son Michael Roberti acts as my research assistant; my beloved husband Paul Roberti not only supports me in all of my endeavors, he taught me everything I know about scuba diving.

CHAPTER ONE

Water-boarding is effective. As Tess was lifted coughing and retching from the makeshift tub, she acknowledged that she was too young to die. By the third immersion she was in and out of consciousness. In a rare moment of lucidity she made peace with her death and remembered that she was the Keeper of the Flame. She had pledged to guard it with her life; apparently the promise was about to come true.

Just as her limbs went slack, she remembered her smart watch. Of course! The men had not thought to take if from her. They had confiscated her cell, briefcase and jacket. Obviously they were not up on the most basic technology. The smart watch monitored her respiration, blood pressure, oxygen levels, pulse and location; it must have been clanging alarm bells back at headquarters.

It really was just functioning as a backup; thanks to nanotechnology she had a tracking device implanted in the curl of the top section of her ear that was virtually undetectable. She studiously avoided looking at the large black object around her wrist as she was dragged from the tub sputtering, gagging and gasping for air.

"Nathan, you son of a bitch, didn't I tell you to wait to question her until I got back from town! Are you trying to kill her before we get the information we need?" Tess could feel the material of a rough blanket being pulled around her, she opened her eyes as a strange man untied her, picked her up and made his way to the back room of the cabin. She struggled as he walked toward the bed.

"Please don't be alarmed Professor Rankin, I won't tie you up. I have brought fresh clothes and toiletries from your home. I'll leave you alone here to rest for a while. I hope you will accept my apologies for the thuggish behavior of my partners." He placed her gently on the bed and walked out.

The minute he left, she groggily pulled herself up and leaned against the door. The cabin walls were logs, but the doors were cheap and thin, she could hear the argument in the living room without any difficulty.

"You idiot! Do you realize what could have happened, then where would we be! It has taken years to locate her! She is our only lead. From now on I will take over the interrogation, you are not thinking clearly." The stranger was shouting at the top of his lungs.

"Listen Avery; don't tell me how long it has been. I'm the one who began the search. I'm the one who brought you in. You better step back before I cut you outta this deal." The man called Nathan was matching the volume of the one named Avery.

Tess was having difficulty placing Nathan's accent. He sounded Russian, but his syntax was very American. She was feeling pretty woozy so she sat down and pulled one of her suitcases toward her. As promised, Avery had packed several changes of clothing; Tess wondered how he had navigated around her state of the art alarm system. She slipped out of her wet things and pulled on black sweats, wincing as she rubbed the ligature marks around her ankles and wrists. Luckily for her, the cabin was very warm. The solid logs that framed the house were acting as a natural insulator.

She pulled her long auburn hair into a ponytail and fastened it with a clip from the bag. At five foot seven and one hundred and forty pounds she was strong and lithe, and with her training, more than a match for any of the Neanderthals that were holding her captive. The argument continued at full volume as she finished with a pair of thick woolen socks and boots.

"Nathan, try not to make threats that you can't back up. You don't move in the circles that I do and you know it. Without my connections you are just another thief with an idea. You are all force and no finesse. She is the perfect example, you are using medieval techniques when I have a bag full of painless alternatives that will give us what we want, but you just blunder ahead without any thought." Avery was cut off in mid shout.

"Listen, Dr. Avery." This was said dripping with sarcasm. "I know just what will crack this bitch." Tess could picture Nathan lightly touching the side of his swollen eye where she had delivered a deeply satisfying kick. She had received a backhand across the face and a cut lip from their first exchange last night when he had attempted to tie her to the bed. Nathan had finally called in Alex and Theo to restrain her while he held a gun to her head. She had slept in that position all night until the early morning dunking.

"What she needs is a little R and R." Tess, having spent most of her life on college campuses, knew that he didn't mean rest and relaxation. Nathan meant Ruffies and rape. The drug Rohypnol, or the "date-rape", drug was the scourge of any campus. The room outside her door went deathly quiet. She was not surprised that Nathan was advocating taking the most brutal approach.

From the first moment she had encountered him, she knew he was a monster. She had been walking to her car after her night class and he had stepped out from behind a van, leveled a gun at her head and told her to drive him to the outskirts of town. He had ordered her to pull off the road and forced her into the trunk. Nathan had been the group's third kidnapping attempt. Tess had played along simply because she didn't have a choice; she had to find out what the men knew about her. Once she ascertained how much of a threat they were, she would decide what to do.

"Look . . . that is not what I signed on for. We are thieves, not . . . not animals. Professor Rankin is a nice lady and she doesn't deserve this kind of treatment. Nathan, we are not going to let you push us around anymore." Alex stammered. Tess had to hand it to him; it took a good deal of courage to stand up to Nathan. He was well over six feet and easily two hundred and fifty pounds of pumped up muscle.

He looked like a cautionary advertisement against steroid use. His head was shaved and his face was pitted with acne scars. He appeared to be about sixty, but it was difficult to tell. He had the voice of a chain smoker and the red mottled nose of a dedicated drinker. The latter fact might work in her favor.

"I believe that I will do whatever I damn well please with the professor and I am guessing that not one of you have the balls to stop me." Nathan's voice had dropped to a menacing growl.

"Nathan stop waving your gun around, we are not impressed. Alex is right, we can get what we want without resorting to assaulting an unconscious woman . . ." Avery was once again interrupted.

"You pansies don't know what you're missing. Believe me, in a few hours she will be begging to tell us what she knows." With this statement Nathan raised his voice and yelled, "Get ready princess, you are about to go for a wild ride." Tess scrambled up from the floor, adrenalin pumping through her veins, as she assumed a fighting stance. She would kill him before he had a chance to touch her.

CHAPTER TWO

Avery spoke in an icily quiet voice. "Nathan, you take one step towards that door and I will blow your brains out all over this cabin." Tess was actually beginning to like Avery. She could picture him going toe to toe with Nathan. From the brief glimpse she had of him he looked forceful. She hoped that Avery would prevail; he seemed to be the lesser of two evils.

Theo chose that moment to chime in. "Look everyone put down their guns and listen to what Avery has to say. We are going to need Professor Rankin to be in good shape in case we have to travel with her. We can't take her any place beaten to a pulp. She will fight us, believe me I know." Tess made a mental note to go easy on Theo when the time came. If they were talking about drugging her she might have to drop the charade sooner than she had anticipated.

"Thank you Theo, finally a reasonable voice. Now I am going to make some food because we can't administer the drug on an empty stomach." Tess could hear Avery moving about in the kitchen, banging pots and pans.

"Nathan I need to tell you what I discovered in town if you will cool off and sit down." Tess heard what sounded like the grunt of a bear and a chair scrapped across the worn lime green linoleum.

Several other chairs were pulled out as she leaned against the door trying to catch every word Avery uttered. "Malcolm is missing. I overheard two cops talking in the diner . . ." Before he could continue Nathan interrupted, it was becoming a pattern.

"What the hell do you mean Malcolm is missing! I thought he had been arrested and was being held without bail in the Jameson jail. People don't just disappear from a jail cell, I would know, I have seen the inside of a few." Nathan sounded a good deal calmer, confused but composed.

"I was just going to tell you what happened. According to the police, Malcolm disappeared the night after they arrested him. They checked his cell during the midnight shift, and in the morning he had vanished. There was not any sign of a break in, and his personal effects as well as his fingerprint cards are also unaccounted for. Apparently the good town of Jameson, Wyoming's fingerprint scan machine is broken so they are temporarily using ink and cards. The deputy in charge of transferring the prints into the computer was participating in a rodeo and they left the cards on his desk . . ." At this point Nathan could not control himself.

"So let me get this straight, Malcolm is gone and the Jameson police don't know who he is or have any way of finding out. He can't be traced to us and the only information they have on him is the fact that he tried to rob the hellcat in there." Tess could only assume he was referring to her. She thought back to the only time she had encountered Malcolm.

It was an uncomfortable memory considering that he had woken her from a deep sleep by shoving a gun in her mouth.   It seemed like a lifetime ago but it had only been four days earlier. She had gone to bed sometime around midnight. The next thing she knew, a strange man was standing over her with a gun resting against her lips. She had immediately slipped her hand under her pillow and switched on her stun gun.

After that, things had moved fairly rapidly, she had him zapped and duck taped before he knew what hit him. After searching the house for her dog Thor, who she discovered unconscious but not injured, she had rung the police and they had taken Malcolm away. She had purposefully played down all aspects of the motive except robbery. The police seemed content to let that be the suspected reason for the break in.

Tess had sent out a message to the Sisterhood after the police left. It might have been a routine crime, but she could not take the chance. The responses were measured but clear. If any other suspicious incident were to happen the council would issue a full alert and a team would be dispatched. The Keeper of the Flame must be protected at all times. Tess had been trained to be ever vigilant. She smiled for the first time in days at the thought of what she assumed had happened to Malcolm.

"You don't think she had anything to do with his disappearance do you?" If she wasn't mistaken Tess thought she heard a slight note of alarm in Nathan's voice. Good, let the monster stew. It would be a while before these jokers figured out that they were in way over their heads, moments after that, they would be dealt with.

"I can't see how that could be possible. She would need a highly professional team to pull off a stunt like that. Alex and I were watching Professor Rankin that night. Remember, it was the next day that we tried to grab her." Tess could picture Theo looking forlornly at his cast.

The ill-fated kidnapping attempt by Alex and Theo had been a cock-up from the beginning. They had approached her outside of the library on the edge of the campus. The University of Wyoming, Jameson branch, was situated in the heart of an ancient forest. That particular section of the campus was heavily wooded. Tess had not been unduly alarmed considering that fact that she had both of the young men in her Monday/Wednesday U.S. Women's History class.

Since school began in September, she had ample time to observe the two brothers. They were Greek, and fell into the dark and handsome (although computer-obsessed) category of students. They invariably wore rock band tee shirts, jeans and well-worn tennis shoes. They would have been virtually indistinguishable if not for the fact that Alex usually sported a neatly trimmed beard.

On the threat assessment scale they registered a zero. That shows how wrong a person can be. Obviously Tess' instincts were not infallible. They had approached her asking innocuous questions about their current paper and she had fallen for the charade. Theo had grabbed her and Alex had attempted to put tape across her mouth.

For their efforts Alex had been kicked in the "sweets", as her British friends would say and Theo had been flipped on his back ending up with his arm facing out at an odd angle. Before they could recover, Tess had bolted back into the library. She assumed the young men had melted into the forest and gone on to seek medical treatment for Theo's arm.

She had not reported the incident to the campus police. Their intervention would not be necessary. She headed home immediately, called headquarters, and then waited to be contacted by the protection team. Tess had been relieved to hear that a retrieval team would not be sent. That would have been premature.

"Dude, don't bring up that humiliating memory. My junk is still sore, I have to hand it to Professor Rankin; she is one tough chick. She's beaten the crap out of everyone but Avery." Alex's voice trailed off as a heartfelt chuckle issued from Avery.

"She is something fierce to behold, I will grant you that. Back to the problem at hand, my guess is that Malcolm found a way to escape the rather primitive jail cell. I would imagine he bribed a lowly deputy. That would explain the lack of evidence and the missing fingerprint cards. Right now we need to focus on getting Professor Rankin to cooperate. With both Malcolm and Professor Rankin missing I assume the sheriff will be scouring the county looking for them." Avery had a point.

Tess realized that an all points bulletin would be issued for she and Malcolm, not any of the others. No one would think to link Alex and Theo to her. The other students probably had not even noticed that they were gone. It could take days before anyone on the campus raised the alarm.

That was for the best; Sheriff Mike was extremely proficient when it came to police work, he also had a vested interest in her, having become something of a father figure after her parents had been killed by a drunk driver when she was sixteen.

"Okay, so let's get going with this miracle drug before this 'isolated' farmhouse is discovered." Now that he had calmed down Nathan was all business.

"Let me bring her out, so far, I am the only person she has not attacked, I suppose I'm due." With another chuckle, heavy footsteps approached her room as Avery opened the door. "Professor Rankin, I am not going to hurt you. I have brought you a peace offering." Tess was astounded to see Thor bounding into her room. As the German Shepherd licked her face she stood up and eyed Avery warily.

"Would you please come out and join us for lunch. I promise that you will not be harmed in any way." Avery put his hand over his heart to add sincerity to his pledge.

"As if I would believe the word of a common criminal." Tess stood her ground, shoulders relaxed but feet apart in case she needed to defend herself. This time Avery laughed out loud. Apparently he found the entire situation very amusing.

"I believe that you will discover that I am much more than a common criminal. I would humbly say that I am rather uncommon when it comes to this type of endeavor. Please come out to the kitchen and join us. You have nothing to fear." He stood to one side as Tess and Thor made their way into the open kitchen/living room.

She approached the table where the rest of the men sat with some trepidation. One on one she could take each of them, even if they were armed. A quick glance reinforced her assessment; Alex and Theo did not have any weapons. Only Avery and Nathan wore belt holsters.

She sat down at the rough-hewn wood plank table. The faint autumnal sun filtered through the windows. Tess looked at the red/orange/gold leaves that were sparsely covering the trees outside and she immediately knew where she was. She had not been able to get her bearings from the bedroom because the windows had been boarded up.

The locals had always referred to the ranch as the Old Miller Place; it was currently owned by an actor who lived in L.A., in the last several years many people "in the industry," as they referred to themselves, had taken a fancy to Wyoming. The locals generally detested them because they drove the housing prices up; complained about the lack of amenities and didn't readily mix with the townsfolk.

"Professor Rankin please eat something, I am sure you are hungry." Avery placed what looked to be some sort of scrambled egg dish in front of Tess.

"I'm not touching anything until I know it's not drugged." Tess eyed the food while Avery leaned over, forked a spoonful off the plate and popped it into his mouth. Tess dug into the food with gusto, not realizing how hungry she was until that moment.

All of the men ate in silence, watching her as if she were a cobra. Avery poured dog food into a bowl and placed it on the floor next to Tess. Thor fell upon the food as if he hadn't eaten in days.

Tess knew that she had to keep up her strength for what was to come. She figured that after lunch the interrogation would begin. Something told her that Avery had a bag of tricks that would breakdown any of the barriers that she had carefully erected since she began her training at sixteen. She knew it was always best to take the initiative.

"I don't know why you brought me here, I have never heard of the Flame of Brazil, I don't even know what it is, and I'm just a history professor at the university. You gentlemen have been sadly misinformed if you think I have something you want." Tess spoke directly to Avery. She wanted to re-enforce his position as the leader, since he seemed the most reasonable.

"Oh Professor Rankin, you are the one who is mistaken, you are exactly what I want." Avery favored her with a grin and a wink.

"See, now you are coming around to my way of thinking . . ." Nathan stood up and took a step toward Tess. Avery grabbed his arm and forced him back into his seat.

"Not now Nathan, after we get the information we need you can have your play time." Tess was rapidly revising her estimation of Avery. Perhaps he was not a reliable man after all. She needed to end this before things progressed beyond her control. She whistled for Thor, stood up and kicked the table over, then bolted for the door.

CHAPTER THREE

With cat-like reflexes, Avery lunged for her and brought her crashing to the floor as Thor attacked Nathan. As his body pressed her shoulder blades against the floor, Avery leveled his gun at her temple. "Call Thor off." He growled through clenched teeth.

"Thor, release." Thor immediately moved to her side as she scrambled up. Nathan was tearing at a bloody rip in his shirt and screaming what she presumed to be curses in Russian. He rushed to the sink and began to clean his wound as Alex brought out a first aid kit.

"Professor Rankin, I want you to sit back down and cooperate or I won't be held accountable for Nathan's actions." Avery ushered Tess to her chair as Nathan eyed Thor with undisguised hatred. She realized that things were unraveling quickly and she still hadn't a clue as to how much the men knew about her. Thus far, all of their questions had been about the Flame, she hoped that they didn't know anything about the Sisterhood.

"Okay, this is how we are going to play this . . ." Avery pulled a chair next to Tess and locked eyes with her. Tess stared back in disgust. "I'm going to give you a drug that will loosen your tongue. It will not hurt you in any way. You will give us the location of the Flame of Brazil and we will drop you and Thor back at your home. If you refuse to work with us, I will turn you over to Nathan and let him use his more primitive methods of persuasion . . ." Avery was cut off by Theo.

"Avery, you can't do that. There would be nothing left of her by the time Nathan was done, please don't . . ." Nathan pushed Theo aside and dropped down in a chair across from Tess.

"Shut the hell up, you cry baby. Avery, give the bitch the drug and let's get going." Tess leaned back to get away from Nathan's odious presence.

"I have never heard of the Flame of Brazil, I have been injured, kidnapped, tied to a bed all night and then tortured by water-boarding. Even with the threat of being drugged hanging over my head I still can't tell you anything." Tess held Avery's steady gaze.

"Professor Rankin, we know who you are. I have been watching you for weeks. Your great-grandmother, grandmother, father and your esteemed self, are the Clan of the Flame. You are the current Keeper, there is no use denying it. Now give me your arm so we may proceed." Avery grabbed her arm and pushed up her sleeve as Alex advanced toward them with a syringe.

Tess was relieved that the men had still not mentioned the Sisterhood. Perhaps they were simply following the heretofore-cold trail of the cursed jewel. She decided to see how powerful a drug they would use; she had been trained to thwart the effects of various 'truth serums'. After all, it would only take seconds for the cavalry to arrive if she hit her retrieval button on the smart watch.

Thor growled and Tess pulled his head into her lap and rubbed it reassuringly. She prepared herself for flight by surreptitiously slipping her left hand around his collar. She rested her right hand in her lap with her finger on the button as Avery inserted the needle. All of the men sat at the table and watched her with fascinated expressions. Avery moved her chair so that his legs were on either side of her.

As Tess looked into his honey colored eyes she realized that he looked familiar. This was the first opportunity that she had to really look at him. There was something about the brown curly hair and athletic build that struck a memory thread. With his broad chest and muscled thighs he reminded her of several skiers she knew. Maybe he was in the campus ski club. No, that was not it.

"Professor Rankin, can you hear me?" Avery's voice was soft and his eyes were concerned. She smiled at him as she realized that he was just her type; well, except for the kidnapping and probable torture part.

"Hey, Avery, I think she kinda likes you. Maybe she is developing Stockholm Syndrome, which could work for us, start oozing charm." Nathan leaned across the table transfixed by the show. Little did he know that it was indeed a show, Tess kept waiting for the drug to take hold; so far nothing was happening. Avery leaned in close and ran his finger down her cheek.

"Professor Rankin, you are not in any danger. I am not going to hurt you. Can you understand what I am saying?" Avery gave her a heartbreaking smile.

"Yes, I can hear you." Tess was astonished with her voice. Her speech was slurred as if she were under the influence of a powerful drug, which didn't make any sense considering the fact that she was very clear headed.

"May I call you Tess?"

"Yes." Tess smiled to further assure Avery that she was cooperating.

"Good, now Tess do you recognize the two young gentlemen sitting across from you?"

"You mean Yogi and Boo Boo?" This elicited an ugly laugh from Nathan. Inwardly Tess was thinking 'Laugh all you want cretin, you will be very sorry by the end of the day'. "Yes I know them; by the way, you two bone heads have failed my course." Avery burst out with an appreciative bark as the two young men protested.

"Now Tess, what about my esteemed colleague Nathan, do you recognize him?" Clearly Avery was expecting another slanderous acknowledgement. Tess did not disappoint him.

"Yes, that is the troglodyte that came up with the water-boarding idea. You will burn in hell for what you have done here today." Tess was afforded a gratifying look of bewilderment from Nathan.

"Hey, what is a troglodyte? Is that some sort of prehistoric animal?" Nathan's bushy uni-brow was furrowed in concentration.

"No comrade it is not an animal, just a cave dweller or a hermit that lives in a hole in the ground." Avery was clearly enjoying the discomfort of his linguistically challenged compatriot. "Now Tess, what about me, do you know who I am?"

"You are an imbecilic moron who has kidnapped the wrong person . . ." Tess' voice trailed off as she really looked at Avery, he had seemed vaguely familiar, then a jolt of recognition hit her so violently that she jumped in her chair. "What in the hell are you doing here? You can't be involved in something like this! My God, you are Dr. Jonathan Avery, the medievalist. You are one of the most respected professors in your field; I have read all of your books. Why are you doing this? You certainly don't need the money." Tess realized that this man was a game changer.

Her extraction team was most certainly in the woods awaiting her signal. She had already decided to spare Alex and Theo, how was she going to dispatch Nathan and contain Avery? He was an internationally recognized expert on medieval history; if the Sisterhood harmed him, governmental agencies would most assuredly become involved.

His presence did not add up. He was wealthy in his own right; he had been a guest lecturer at Stanford, Cambridge and most recently in Mumbai. Perhaps it was simply the thrill of the chase. Everyone loved a treasure hunt. He was correct; he was a very uncommon criminal.

"I am deeply gratified that you recognize me. Thank you for being an appreciative fan. Please feel free to call me Jack. Now that we are all familiar and relaxed I would like to talk about your job . . ." Nathan interrupted by mumbling several profanities under his breath as Avery, aka Jack, proceeded. "Would you please tell me what classes you teach?" Jack leaned forward and locked eyes with Tess as if he were trying to warn her of something, Tess really could not understand the dynamic, however she didn't see any harm in this line of questioning as long as she was careful.

"I was hired two years ago so I only teach the U.S. History survey courses." She hoped that would be vague enough.

"Right, now can you be a bit more specific. Are these general history courses or are they specialized in any way?" Jack seemed genuinely interested in her answers, even though she knew full well that if he had been watching her for weeks, as he had claimed, he would know every class she was teaching for the fall semester.

According to the cat clock on the wall he had been questioning her for over twenty minutes and still his vaunted truth serum had not kicked in. Aside from the slurring she had not noticed any side effects. That was decidedly odd.

"I have three general U.S. History courses and two sections of U.S. Women's History." She was alarmed to notice that his eyes narrowed in concentration when she mentioned her Women's History courses.

"Now we are getting somewhere, in your Women's History courses I assume you spend a great deal of time on the women's suffrage movement?" With this question Tess knew where he was headed. It was time to obfuscate.

"Sure, I cover it in both sections. As Alex and Theo have learned, the official date for the beginning of the women's rights movement in the U.S. can be traced back to the first women's rights convention formed by Elizabeth Cady Stanton and Lucretia Mott on July 19 & 20, 1848 in Seneca Falls, New York. Stanton and Mott had first met in June of 1840 at the World Anti-Slavery Convention held in London. Stanton was on her honeymoon with her husband Henry and Mott was one of only six women delegates . . ." Now it was her turn to be interrupted.

"Avery this is a load of bull, just get to the point before we all die of boredom." Nathan rose and began to pace the small kitchen. Tess smiled inwardly. She had Nathan just where she wanted him, aggravated and distracted. She hoped he would not notice the subtle shift that had occurred in the line of questioning.

Every time Tess had been about to reveal something of importance Jack had slightly shifted in his chair, as if in warning. He seemed to be signaling that he was on her side. At this juncture she really couldn't tell.

"Nathan, will you shut the hell up. Let me do this at my own pace. Why don't you go outside and walk around for a bit to cool off." Jack's eyes were following Nathan's agitated form.

"Oh, please continue, I wouldn't want to miss out on the history lesson about a bunch of castrating old harpies fighting for their right to vote. Right to vote! What a waste! Women are only useful as cooks and bed warmers . . ." For the first time Nathan was interrupted. Tess was more than happy to put an end to his sexist tirade.

"For your information comrade, your country was one of the earliest to grant women the right to vote in 1917." She leveled what she hoped to be a withering glance toward Nathan as he slumped into a chair at the end of the table farthest from her.

"Wait, how do you know I am Russian? I didn't tell you that." Nathan seemed to under the misapprehension that he could successfully disguise his accent.

"Oh, please, it is so obvious. Now where was I? Before the conference began several men had voted to seat the women attendees in a segregated section out of the sight of men. The irony of this decision at an anti-slavery convention did not seem to occur to them. Stanton was so angry that she could not see Mott's speech that she promptly introduced herself and they struck up a history making friendship." Tess smiled obligingly at Jack as if she were his star pupil.

"Stanton returned home and eventually moved to Seneca Falls, New York where she began to lobby the New York state legislature for married women's rights. In 1848, New York passed a bill that gave wives control over their inheritance, not their wages. As I said, that same year Stanton, Mott and Mott's sister Martha organized the convention to discuss the 'social, civil and religious condition of women'." Tess abruptly stopped her history lesson to see if it was having the intended effect. Apparently not, Jack looked riveted.

"Now Tess, if I remember it correctly this is the convention that drafted the Declaration of Rights and Sentiments, which was based on the Declaration of Independence. I know that several resolutions were put before the three hundred attendees and one was a resolution supporting women's suffrage. It narrowly passed by a small margin. In 1851 Stanton met Susan B. Anthony and they began their historic fifty-year partnership. One evening Alex explained to us that Stanton and Anthony went on to form the National Woman Suffrage Association in New York City in 1869. Now the question I have for you is what was happening across the pond? Were British women agitating for their right to vote?" Game, set and match; Jack had her right where he wanted her.

Tess tried to keep her mind from racing. She had to provide them with an answer that would not give away the Sisterhood's existence. She processed all of the information she had gleaned from their various conversations. Thus far they had taunted her with the fact that they knew about the Flame of Brazil and that she was the Keeper of the Flame.

She could not see that it would do any real damage to acknowledge that fact. As Jack was creeping closer to his ultimate revelation she had to throw them something, anything to keep them off the track of her organization.

"Now Tess, it is time to stop prevaricating and tell us the truth. My companions and I are growing tired of your charade." Jack leaned toward her as Tess looked out the window.

The light was beginning to fade as an early dusk settled over the mountains. Tess had two choices; she could end the interrogation now or try to hang on a bit longer to see if they had any more information that she needed. She decided to gamble.

She tried to say "fine" but it came out sounding like "shine". Obviously the drug was still in her system but she could not feel any clouding of her perceptions.

"You are correct, before the turn of the century British women were agitating for the right to vote, same as in the United States." Tess stopped to see how far he would press.

"Good, now according to Theo, by that time Carrie Chapman Catt, Harriett Stanton Blach, who was Elizabeth Cady Stanton's daughter, and the Reverend Anna Shaw were leading the suffrage movement in the U.S. Who was the leading figure in Great Britain?" As Jack finished Nathan jumped up from the table and began to stride toward Tess.

"And now comes the time for truth. We all know that Emmeline Pankhurst and her daughters were the undisputed leaders of the group of whores that were little more than terrorists. Your great-grandmother, Sara Jones, ran away from her family in Wales and joined their gaggle in London!" Nathan was yelling as he approached her with a menacing look.

"She armed herself with explosives and killed my grandfather!" Now all of the pieces began to fall into place, Nathan's heritage and his undisguised hatred of her, their knowledge of the Flame and the fact that no one had mentioned Nathan's last name, which was Bukharin. It was time for Tess to push him over the edge.

"Jack is right, let's all stop playing cat and mouse. I am proud to acknowledge that I am the great-granddaughter of Sara Jones. She was a heroine. Her most notable achievement was killing this gorilla's grandfather. My only regret was that he had managed to sire a son before he was removed." Tess' words had their desired effect.

Nathan lunged toward her as Jack tried in vain to impede the raging man's progress. Nathan tackled her with the full force of his bull like body. Tess felt the chair fall from under her, then nothing.

CHAPTER FOUR

Tess regained consciousness lying on a couch in the living room. She gingerly slipped her hand behind her head to inspect the egg size, rhythmically throbbing lump. Thor sympathetically licked her face as she struggled to pull herself up to a sitting position. Other than a headache and the injury, she seemed to be in one piece.

She glanced around to ascertain if she and Thor were alone in the living room. Male voices could be heard out on the front porch, but the room seemed to be deserted. She pressed several buttons on her smart watch, which sent the message, "OK, stand by, retrieve soon."

"Why would you do that Tess? Why push him? You know that I am barely keeping him in check." She jumped as Jack's voice reached out from the shadows near the fireplace.

"Why drug me with a substance that keeps my mind clear, who in the hell are you working for?" Tess swung her legs off the couch and walked toward Jack.

"I'll just bet that your friends don't know your real agenda. I think you are playing all of us, maybe I should suggest that to the others and see how they react."

Jack moved out of the shadows revealing a nasty swollen eye. "I don't think you want to push Nathan any further. You are lucky to be alive. I can't figure out why you continue to bait him. It doesn't result in anything but injuries for the two of us. Can't you see that I am trying to protect you; just give us the information and we will let you go."

Tess warily watched Jack as he went into the kitchen and prepared two sandwiches and poured each of them a glass of milk. "Sit down and eat something before he gets back from his walk. Let's hope he has calmed down by now, it took the three of us to restrain him after that stunt you pulled. God Tess, how you try my patience."

"Well I wouldn't want to do that, after all you have been so kind to me, what with the smacking around and the kidnapping." Sarcasm dripped from each word as Tess ate her food, pausing to share sections of the sandwich with Thor. "I don't know why we are dancing around this Jack. We both know I am not going to tell you anything. This is just a waste of time."

"No this is not a waste; I am trying to convince you that I am on your side before . . ." Jack was interrupted by the sound of raised voices as Nathan burst through the door, followed closely by Theo and Alex.

"Well now isn't this a cozy tableau, see professor I know a few fancy words too. Okay, you are up and ready and I have cooled off." Nathan reached the table and stood menacingly over Tess.

"Avery I suggest you up the dosage for this next round. I want her to be completely helpless when I get my turn at her." Nathan patted her on the head as he dropped down in a chair across the table, "And put that mangy cur outside." Alex opened the door and she gave Thor the order. She needed him outside when she made her escape.

Jack administered another dose as Tess quickly realized that this injection was benign. With his back to the other men, Jack had mouthed, "be ready." Tess had taken this as a confirmation that, as she had suspected, he had another agenda. She needed to get the others out of the way and focus on him.

As before, Jack sat in front of her with his legs on either side. "Now Tess, we know you believe your great-grandmother was a heroine. We have all seen the film Iron Jawed Angels, we know that women fought and died for the right to vote. In the U. S. the women were called suffragists, in England they were called suffragettes, can you tell me a bit about those ladies?"

Tess knew that this was her cue to begin a story that would lead Nathan to his final goal. Unfortunately for him, he would not benefit from this knowledge. "My great-nana Sara was from Wales." Tess slurred her words and slowly closed, then opened her eyes, attempting to mimic a drug induced state. "She was sixteen when she ran away to London in 1907 and joined the WSPU."

Nathan began to grumble under his breath about the suffragettes, as Tess inwardly smiled. Alex and Theo leaned forward, while Jack picked up the thread. "Yes, yes, we know that Sara joined the Women's Social and Political Union formed by Emmeline Pankhurst and her daughters Christabel, Sylvia and Adela. What can you tell us about the WSPU's decision to switch to more violent actions to make their point?"

"No, no. It was not Sara's fault! She was just following orders! It was because of Alfred Nobel!" Tess was rather enjoying this wild goose chase.

"Okay Tess, now you have lost us. What does Alfred Nobel have to do with Sara?" Jack's slight smile and the amused twinkle in his eye were not observable to his compatriots because of his position.

"Alfred Nobel was born in Stockholm, Sweden on October 21, 1833 . . ." Tess' sing-song litany was interrupted by a low growl emanating from deep within Nathan's throat, which abruptly ceased with her next sentence.

"He moved with his family to St. Petersburg, Russia when he was nine." Nathan leaned forward as she continued her story.

"As an adult Nobel became an engineer and inventor. After spending a good deal of time around construction sites he became interested in the slow process of blasting rocks. In 1860 he began to experiment with nitroglycerin, which was a highly unstable liquid invented by the Italian chemist Ascanio Sobrero in 1846." Even as she enjoyed rattling off inconsequential facts gleaned from Google, Tess knew her time was limited.

"Go on." Jack stood up and began to turn on lights around the room. The night had descended without the assembled group even noticing.

"In 1863 he invented the blasting cap and by 1866 he discovered that when he mixed nitroglycerine with silica he had created dynamite." With the mention of dynamite, Nathan sat straight up.

"So with the invention of dynamite, Nobel became a millionaire and when he died he left his entire fortune to a foundation which awards prizes every year to people who help humanity in some way." Jack wrapped up the lecture. "However, the interesting part of your story is that fact that dynamite is used for blasting rock, for example, one might use it in the mining field. I believe that Sara came from a mining family in Wales."

All eyes were on Tess as she dejectedly nodded her head in agreement. Jack sat back down in front of her and took her firmly by the shoulders. "Tess, are you telling us that Sara learned how to use dynamite from her father and she was recruited by the WSPU as some sort of terrorist?"

As Thor began to excitedly bark outside, Tess realized her time was up; the extraction team was in place. Somehow she had to neutralize Nathan, keep Alex and Theo out of harm's way and contain Jack. Her mind was racing in its attempt to find a solution, while she slowly got to her feet feigning a grogginess that she did not feel.

"No, it was not like that, Sara was not a terrorist. She was just a young girl who was willing to give her life for the suffrage cause." Tess began to step back slowly toward the front windows. All of the men stood up and watched her seemingly innocuous progress. Nathan pulled a gun from behind his back and advanced on her. Jack made a movement to stop him, but he was shoved roughly aside.

"Back off pretty boy, she is mine now. You have had your fun. So Tess, you admit that your great-grandmother knew how to handle dynamite and that she was part of a militant faction of the WSPU. Everyone in this room knows that Sara planted the dynamite on the tracks, blew up my grandfather's train and then stole the Flame of Brazil off his dead body." Nathan followed the retreating Tess as she positioned him perfectly in front of the windows.

"Now you are going to tell us where the Flame is or I will blow out both of your kneecaps." With that declaration Nathan leveled the gun at her right knee. Tess raised her hands in mock supplication.

"Okay Nathan you win. Sara inadvertently killed your grandfather when she blew up the train tracks. It was a horrible accident, it was not a passenger train and she didn't expect to hurt anyone. She noticed the satchel chained to your grandfather's wrist and she took it, when she opened it later she found the largest ruby in the world, the Flame of Brazil. I am the Keeper of the Flame and I have it back at my ranch in a safe." Tess flashed a warning look to Jack.

He must have understood her motion because he grabbed Alex and Theo by their arms and backed away from the front of the cabin. Nathan stood with his back to them and did not notice their strategic retreat. "Finally, I knew you would eventually come to your senses. Now give the boys the location and combination of your safe and we can spend some time together in the back room."

Nathan leveled his gun at her head and moved to the center of the picture windows; he was perfectly positioned. "Fine get some paper and write it down, I will gladly turn myself over to Jack, not you." Tess made the universal sign for surrender by crossing her wrists in front of her body. As she did so, she pushed a button on her smart watch.

There was a faint cracking sound as Tess yelled, "Down", and hit the floor. Nathan's head exploded in a mass of bone and tissue. His lifeless body swayed as a red mist of blood fell around him, then slumped to the floor. The rapid repeat of gunfire erupted around the cabin as all of the lights were shattered. An eerie quiet enveloped the inhabitants until Jack whispered.

"Jesus, Mary and Joseph, Tess, are you okay?" He belly crawled toward her and gathered her in his arms. "Did you do that?"

"No, obviously I don't have a gun. My retrieval team took him out. Now let go of me so I can signal the all clear and leave. I will make sure no one comes in here. Get Alex and Theo as far from here as possible." Tess attempted to untangle herself from Jack's iron grip.

"Like hell I will. Alex and Theo get over here." The boys did as they were told. With one agile leap Thor jumped through the broken window and rushed to her side. Jack pulled out his gun and pointed it at her; with his free hand he reached in his pocket, brought out Tess' cell phone, and handed it to her.

"Get them on the phone and tell them to stand down, now!" Jack yelled as Tess pressed the number.

"This is Keeper Three; I am ok, stand down, repeat, stand down." Tess pulled herself to a sitting position studiously ignoring the mass of blood and gore that used to be the odious Nathan. She had a brief moment to register the fact that she was not sorry he was dead as she brushed bits of brain matter off her clothes. "Now what Captain Jack, do you have a plan?"

"As a matter of fact I do, tell your cohorts that we will be leaving in my Jeep. I want them to promise no harm will come to Alex and Theo. When we get a bit of distance and I know they are safe I will let you go." Jack carefully watched Tess as she relayed the message to her team.

"Done, they have no reason to hurt the guys." Tess handed the phone back to Jack, who promptly smashed it under foot.

"Good, now take off your smart watch and Thor's collar, then get your luggage from the bedroom." Tess did as she was told with Jack on her heels. She could hear retching from the living room as she gathered up her things. Without thinking she hugged Alex and Theo good-bye as they mumbled their apologies.

"Now walk in front of me until we get to the car and then you will sit in the driver's seat." Jack wrapped his arm around her and pressed his gun against her temple. Tess moved to the Jeep, tossed her luggage in back and let Thor into the back seat. She got behind the wheel as Jack, using the car as cover, joined her in the front.

Engines turned over and lights appeared as they drove onto the main road, however, they did not see any lights behind them. Tess knew there would be no need, she was sure that a tracking device had been attached to the vehicle and she had her implant as a backup.

In her estimation the situation could not have been better. Nathan was neutralized and she only had one person to deal with, now she just needed to find out who Jack worked for and how much that agency knew about the Sisterhood.

"So CIA, FBI, NSA, Homeland Security; which one of those agencies planted a mole in a gang of jewel thieves?" Tess turned onto the main highway away from Jameson as Jack motioned to the left. A rich robust burst of laughter emanated from Jack as he lowered his gun and turned to view her.

"Oh, Tess you are so naïve, I don't work for any agency. I am in this for the Flame, of course the people I am taking you to do work for the U. S. government in a capacity that they can explain." Jack reached his hand forward and began to run his fingers through her ponytail.

This was taking a decidedly worrisome turn. The fact that Jack was sexually attracted to her would work in her favor; however, she would not be able to exploit it if she were turned over to another group. Her mind was racing calculating the odds of when she should just bolt. "But I thought you were in charge." It was always a good idea to feed a person's vanity.

"No Tess, we are going to meet the only people who have any influence over me, my mom and dad."

CHAPTER FIVE

"What in the hell has been going on around here, I leave you all for a couple of days and the place falls apart. A damn rodeo, that's all it was. An out of town rodeo and you manage to have a jail break, two missing persons and a kidnapping!" Sheriff Mike de Haan furiously approached his two deputies. The shiny black cowboy boots added to his already impressive six-foot four inches. Combining the height with a linebacker build, still in fighting form, and the spit and polish of his uniform, he was a formidable presence.

The female deputy moved toward the sheriff; even at five foot eleven, she was dwarfed by his size. She ran her fingers through a short golden blonde bob and fixed her furious blue eyes on her superior. She squared her shoulders as if readying for a blow.

"Look dad, do you think we have just been sitting around on our butts! Tess is my best friend! From what we have seen on the campus camera she was kidnapped at gunpoint! Gunpoint! As if that was not bad enough, the guy that broke into her house has disappeared into thin air and two

of her students are missing! How is any of this our fault?"
She was pulled away by the other deputy as the sheriff
advanced.

"Sorry Deb . . .okay I don't mean to yell and blame you
and Edward. Let's all just sit down and figure this out."
Edward pulled out a chair for Deb as the sheriff dejectedly
dropped into his chair behind his desk. He looked at his
distraught daughter and remembered happier days when
Tess, Deb and Edward had spent most of their time on the
town's soccer fields.

At six feet and two hundred pounds of pure muscle,
Edward had earned the respect of the soccer coach and the
entire team. That was no mean feat considering the fact that
Edward was the only African American kid in Jameson. He
had gone away to Ohio State and chosen to return to their
little town for only one reason, Deb.

"Alright, I am sorry; it's just that this is more action than
we have in a year. Look I have notified the FBI about Tess'
kidnapping and they are sending an agent who should be here
soon. As for the two students, we are working with the
university on that. I do want to talk about the missing prisoner
with Mason; he was on duty. Where is he by the way?" Mike
looked around the station.

The building itself was constructed of faded red brick. The front door was beveled glass with the words Jameson Sheriff's Department inscribed in black. As you entered there were several decrepit wooden chairs placed against walls that were covered in old maps of Wyoming and paintings that featured covered wagons, massive bison and running horses.

A low wooden wall separated the waiting room from the assembled desks. A person entered the work area by pushing through a set of short swinging doors. Mike had a small, enclosed office behind the six oak desks that faced the front door. Other doors to the right led to four cells and the restrooms.

Edward shifted uncomfortably in his chair. "Well sir, he's still at the rodeo. We left a message on his cell, but he has not picked up. Deb and I have been over to Tess' place and checked in with the ranch foreman, he has organized a search party and his guys have been all over this county, nothing to report."

"Listen dad, we tried to run the plates on the car we saw Tess forced into, but they were conveniently covered in mud. We are circulating a photo of the vehicle around to the other law enforcement agencies in the state, again nothing." Deb got up and walked to the bank of windows behind her father. "I pray to God we find her alive."

Mike turned in his chair, stood up and rested his big hands on her shoulders. "Don't worry, we will find her and bring her home. Gun or no gun Tess is a match for any man. We need to fan out and look for that car on every back road in the county. Edward where is your mother? We need her to hold down the fort while we are gone."

"I can't say, she has been MIA all afternoon. Man, first Mason and now my mom, we can't even locate our own people. Should we ask Robyn to come in? She could bring the baby." Edward's hand was poised over his cell as Mike gave the nod, Edward walked out of the room to make the call.

Mike could remember the days when the department didn't have such complicated leave schedules. A guy would take off a few days when his wife had a baby or he went on a fishing/hunting trip. They even had a male dispatcher; of course he was the meanest S. O. B. who had ever drawn breath. The day he retired was one of the happiest of Mike's life. The very next morning Mrs. Robinson came in dragging a scrawny little Edward along behind.

Mike had hired her on the spot. Because she was from the south everyone in town fell to calling her Miz Robinson. She had such a regal way about her that no one would have dared call her by her given name. The only mention of a Mr. Robinson had been a brief reference to a

49

gunshot wound; no one had ever summoned the courage to inquire any further.

Now the department was equally split between Mason, Edward, Deb and Robyn, whom was off on maternity leave. Robyn Ito was born into a prominent local Vietnamese family; her husband Jeff's family was Japanese, one of several, which had settled in Jameson when they had been released from the Heart Mountain Internment Camp after WWII.

Many of the Japanese families had lost everything when they were interned. The Ito's lost their home and tutoring business, Jeff's grandparents had been professors; and they were promptly hired by the University of Wyoming upon their release.

Mike might have been the sheriff but everyone knew that Miz Robinson was the glue that held everything together. "Alright Deb, we are going to get Robyn in here and then we will split up and look for Tess. Baby, don't worry, I know we will find her."

Just as Deb turned to her dad, Edward raced into the office. "Sir, I have Tess' foreman on the line and he says one of his men heard shots fired at the Old Miller Place. When he went to investigate he said it looked like the OK Corral. He found the car we were looking for and a body . . ." Deb began to sway as Edward reached for her.

"No babe, it's not Tess, they think it might be the guy who grabbed her. Apparently, his head was blasted almost clean off his body." Edward handed his phone to Mike as Miz Robinson arrived.

"What in the name of Moses is goin' on around here? Son, I can hear you out in the street." Miz Robinson calmly moved to her desk and gracefully placed her six-foot frame into her chair.

Patting her perfect coal black chignon she slipped off her coat and positioned it around the chair's back. It was as if the captain had taken the helm. "Do you want to tell me what has got you so all fired up?"

"Sorry ma' am, we think we have a lead on Tess." Edward moved aside as Mike approached the front of the station.

"Evening, Miz Robinson, thank heaven you're here. We are heading out to the Old Miller Place and we need you to handle everything while we are gone."

"Why Sheriff Mike, you know I can do that. Run along and may the Lord and all his angels go with you." Miz Robinson began to work on her computer as Edward ran over to give her a quick kiss on the cheek before they headed out.

Mike and Deb got into the front of the squad car, while Edward jumped in the back. Just as they prepared to turn out of the driveway, the tall, lanky, sandy-haired deputy came running up on foot. "Sorry Sheriff, my truck broke down and my cell quit on me."

"Forget about that now Mason, get in and we will explain what has happened along the way." For the next several minutes the officers exchanged information, discussed the various cases they were working and tried to tie all of the seemingly disparate events together, all talking ground to a halt when Mike pulled up in front of the Miller home, leaving his lights on for illumination.

"Gregg what in heck fire happened here? This looks like something out of an L.A. gang war." Mason approached Tess' foreman, Gregg Redhawk, as Edward, Deb and Mike walked up the steps and peered into the darkened cabin, shining their flashlights around the room.

Gregg pushed back his cowboy hat and ran his hand across his mouth. "Well, I can't say what happened. Tess isn't here but the car we were looking for, and I believe the man that took her are. I went inside when my man called and looked at the body, don't worry, I didn't touch anything. That fella is missing most of his head and bugs are everywhere, luckily we got here before any animals had at him."

Mike looked out into the darkened forest; if Tess had fought her killer and managed to escape she would have made her way to the road and walked back into town.

That means they would have seen her on the way out. Deb whispered the question that was on all of their lips.

"If he is dead, where is Tess?" Where indeed?

CHAPTER SIX

"Stay on Interstate 25 until we get to Buffalo and then pull off at the gas station where Interstate 90 and Route 16 intersect." Jack had obviously been to northern Wyoming before, he was rattling off instructions without the benefit of a map or GPS.

"How about we take Route 16 West and drive to Thermopolis, then onto the Wind River Reservation? We could visit Sacajawea's gravesite." Tess turned a smirking face to Jack.

"Give it a rest Tess; I am still trying to process all of your elucidating info about the Bighorn Mountains to the west and the Thunder Basin National Grasslands to the east." Jack cast an exasperated look her way.

"Okay, have it your way, you will now miss out on my fascinating story of how the Crazy Woman River got its name." Tess had been baiting him the entire car ride. It was better to keep him off kilter, if gave her a decided advantage.

They continued on in silence until they reached the turn off. As instructed, Tess parked in the back of the station next to a large black truck. Jack shifted people, luggage and faithful hound into the new car. Tess was traveling north on Interstate 90 outside of Sheridan when she spoke up.

"I just wanted to point out that we will be crossing the border into Montana in a few minutes. When we get into the Custer National Forest and cross through the Crow Reservation, should I stay on 90 or take Route 212 through the Northern Cheyenne Reservation?" Tess favored Jack with her ever-helpful smile.

"Stay on 90, go through Billings and head west toward Bozeman, we will turn on Route 89 when we hit the Lewis and Clark National Forest." Jack lapsed back into a morose contemplation of the road ahead.

"Nice truck, it handles really well for being such a big fella." Tess was trying to decide how best to approach the question of what would happen when they arrived at their destination.

"The other car was a rental that I picked up in Casper, this is mine. We needed to switch because I was absolutely sure that your team had attached tracking devices to all the cars that were parked by the cabin." Jack briefly turned to look her way, and then with a sigh, he returned to staring out the windshield.

They passed several dark hours in silence until they reached Springdale and made the turn north onto Route 89 toward White Sulphur Springs. "So I take it you are not a night person. May I at least ask what is going to happen to me when we get to your parents' home?" Tess attempted to add a slight catch in her voice to gain his sympathy.

"Sorry I haven't had much sleep in the last couple of days. Nothing is going to happen to you, the U. S. government does not make a habit of torturing innocent civilians. We will try to persuade you to cooperate with us. I believe once you hear our arguments you will agree to turn over the Flame. You are in great danger; we don't know who Nathan told about you. You must give us the Flame or you will be hunted for the rest of your life." Jack turned pleading eyes toward Tess.

"Look Jack, you know I don't have it in my safe at home. I'm not going to insult your intelligence by denying everything you already know. My family used to be the Keepers, now the Sisterhood just stores all of its assets in a Swiss bank account. We are what we purport to be, an organization that protects women and children all over the world. " Tess tried for a level tone of sincerity.

"Oh, Tess, I wish I could believe you, but I don't, I have memorized the history of your organization and I have been watching you for weeks, if you don't have it, you know where it is." He put up his hand as she began to argue the fact.

"Tess, when I say I know you I mean it. I know all about Deb, you and Edward, your favorite foods, movies you like, what time you go to sleep, when you wake up, hell I even know when you are starting your . . . wait turn in here." Jack gestured to a small dirt roadway on the left.

Tess had just enough time to read a little sign that said something about the Sixteenmile River. They bumped along on a road that resembled a goat path for about half a mile until they reached a clearing in the forest. Tess pulled into a circular driveway of an enormous log cabin. "Wow, what do your parents do for a living?"

"My dad is a physicist at Montana State University in Bozeman, that's where he met my mom, she's a chemist. Of course now she's . . ." Tess finished his sentence for him.

"Oh man, I knew there was something important about your parents; your mom is Senator Avery. Right, now the connection to the government makes sense." Tess and Jack got out of the car and released Thor, who went bounding off into the forest. "I'm not really in any shape to meet your folks. Could we put off the interrogation until I've had some sleep?"

"No problem, they are not here. They have graciously given me forty-eight hours to try and get you to cooperate. You better call Thor; we have bears in these parts." Jack escorted Tess and Thor into his home. The front entrance and living room were open to the top of the house with a huge two story stone fireplace dominating the room.

"Wow this is really cozy, what with the dead animal heads everywhere." As he began to growl, Tess pulled Thor away from a taxidermied Grizzly bear.

"Very funny, look who's talking you grew up in Wyoming. Don't let the intellectual sheen of academia fool you, I am a native son of Montana, I fish, hunt, ride and am a fairly accurate shot." Jack motioned Tess toward the back of the house to a massive kitchen. "Are you hungry?"

"No, but Thor could use some water." Tess watched Jack move around the well-provisioned kitchen. The stainless steel appliances gleamed and there was fresh fruit in several bowls on the butcher-block island. Obviously Jack had been back to stock up. That meant he had planned on somehow ridding them of his three fellow conspirators.

"Okay, while Thor drinks, I am sure you want to take a shower. You have Nathan's blood all over you. Come with me to my room." Jack led her upstairs, pointed out his sisters' and parents' rooms; then walked to the end of the hall. They entered into a small library/sitting room, then moved into the main section of the bedroom which was dominated by a king-sized four poster bed made of highly glossed walnut.

"That was my great-grandparent's bed; my grandfather, mother, sisters and I were all conceived in that bed. Someday it will be my kids turn." Jack gave her an inscrutable look.

"Well Jack, I have to say that is kind of cool and creepy at the same time. I hope at least you have changed the mattresses after all of the begetting." Much to Tess' surprise Jack's laughter echoed through the room.

"You never disappoint Tess, come on." He led her into a bathroom with gorgeous tile and a two-person shower. "Now I am going to stay in here with you, because I don't trust you. The shower doors are frosted so you don't have to worry about your maidenly virtue." Jack pulled up a chair from the sitting room, as Tess hung her towel over the side of the shower and stepped in.

She pulled off her soiled clothes and threw them over the side. The hot water and dozens of pulsing jets soothed her stress strained muscles. She took the time to contemplate her situation, she knew that Jack was attracted to her and that would work in her favor.

His parents had given them two days, in which she assumed he would try the soft approach, sort of like "romancing the stone", away from her. She had used the term "Sisterhood" and he had acknowledged he already knew about the organization.

It was imperative that she discovered everything he knew regarding the Sisterhood and the Flame; then she needed to attempt an escape. God, but she was tired, the hot shower and the fact that it was the middle of the night, suddenly hit her at full force. She finished washing her hair: toweled off, pulled on a flannel nightshirt and joined Jack and Thor in the bedroom.

Jack had changed into a tee shirt and sweat pants and he still held the gun. He was seated on a chair facing the bed; Thor had stretched out in his usual spot on the right of the mattress. Tess snuggled into the left side and turned off the bedside light. As she punched the feather pillows into compliance Jack spoke in the darkness.

"Did you send a kill order for Nathan?"

"No, I positioned him with his gun arm facing the window so they could shoot him there. He was no use to us dead, were your people out there? Maybe they saw the gun and they panicked." She answered truthfully.

"That's not possible, our guys were told to stay away from the entire area, for fear that they would tip off the Sisterhood."

"Jack, I can't say I'm sorry he is dead, the thought of that monster touching me gives me chills, but we don't just go around killing people for no reason. It was a retrieval team, not a hit squad."

"Tess you have to believe me when I say that I wouldn't have let him hurt you. The water-boarding incident should never have happened, I'm sorry, I believe you regarding Nathan's death. So if it wasn't either of our people, who else could have wanted Nathan dead?"

"You tell me, you seem to know a good deal more than I do about the actors in this drama." Tess shifted in bed.

"Well, let's see, besides the U. S. government, it could be Russia, the U. K., Brazil, Portugal or India." Jack spoke into the darkened room.

"Wait, what? I understand all of those countries might have jurisdiction over the Flame, but how do India and Portugal come into this?" Tess questioned.

"Tess I am too wiped out now to explain what I discovered when I worked at the university in Mumbai. I will

tell you everything tomorrow, I promise, now go to sleep."
Jack sounded weary to the bone.

Sometime in the night Jack climbed into bed, stretched his arm around her stomach and pulled her backwards against his chest. "Sorry, I couldn't resist."

Tess relaxed against him and he sighed. She knew this was the perfect opportunity to get Jack on her side. When his parents arrived she wanted to have Jack's allegiance; pretending to be cooperative and docile could only work in her favor. She had to move quickly if she wanted to convince Jack that she needed a protector against a united parental onslaught. Poor guy, he would never know how efficiently he had been manipulated; at least not until it was all over.

"It's okay; just don't get any funny ideas. Hey, does it matter to you that I didn't have anything to do with Nathan's death?" Tess asked.

"Yes." Was Jack's short reply.

"Why?"

"It just does."

"One last question, is that your gun or are you . . .?" Tess was cut off by his, now familiar, deep-throated laughter.

"God, you will be the death of me, just go to sleep you vixen." Tess promptly dropped into one of the deepest night's sleep she had ever experienced.

CHAPTER SEVEN

Tess awoke to the soft autumnal light streaming through the trees into the window. The clock on the bedside table read eleven as Jack entered the room carrying a steaming tray of food, Thor bounded in behind him. "Why are you always trying to feed me?" Tess enquired as she propped herself up on the pillows.

Jack settled the tray on her lap and joined her in bed, bracing himself against the footboard facing her. "Well, you are a bit on the skinny side. I think it's a combination of eating mostly soups and salads. You could use a little more meat on your bones."

"I am not skinny, I am lean. Hey what is this? It's very tasty." Tess indecorously shoveled mouthfuls of food into her while Jack rattled on.

"I call it Jack's Special; it's scrambled eggs, sausage, cubed hash browns, onions, garlic, pepper and a secret ingredient that I won't tell you. Thor loves it." At the mention of his name Thor jumped on the bed and placed his head in Jack's lap.

"What's up with that? I can't figure out how a one-person guard dog has so readily adapted to you." Tess shook her head at Thor, who closed his eyes as Jack rubbed the sweet spot behind his ears.

"Please don't blame poor old Thor, he was reluctant at first, but food won him over. Alex and Theo figured out how to disarm your alarm and I went into your house everyday and snooped around. Between the daily ham offering and the fact that you weren't home to protect, he soon relaxed. I even used to take him out for a run if your foreman or ranch hands were not around." Jack continued to familiarly pet Thor.

"Look Jack, I appreciate the food, if not the fact that you are a government supported stalker, but you honestly can't believe that I am going to give you the location of the Flame. The intel that several agencies, from various counties, are searching for the Flame does not mean that I'm running scared, that has been an issue for over one hundred years." Tess finished her food as Jack slowly shook his head.

"No Tess, you are quite wrong about the present situation, Nathan found several dossiers concerning Sara when he was cleaning out his late father's house. He took them to a researcher at the university library in Moscow. She pieced together the story and now the Russians are searching for Sara's ancestors. I only found out about this when I stumbled upon the researcher's name while I was looking into the history of the Flame . . . " Tess jumped at the new information.

"Wait, so you were researching the Flame and you found someone else using the same search engines? But can't the Russians just reverse that and come after you?" Tess placed her fork carefully on her plate and wondered why the thought of Jack being hunted was so disconcerting.

"That's what happened, I was a guest lecturer at the university in Mumbai and I stumbled upon information about the Flame when I was researching the Taj Mahal. That night I arrived back at my apartment to find two burly looking characters tearing the place apart." Jack stood up, picked up the tray and headed for the door.

"You probably want to take a shower and get dressed. The windows are nailed shut and I will be right outside the door if . . ." He turned as Tess jumped off the bed.

"But, what happened? What did you do when you found the guys in your apartment?"

"Well, I ran, of course. I had lived in Mumbai for a year and I knew every twist and turn of every back alley in my neighborhood. They didn't find anything because I had all my research on my laptop. I went straight to the U. S. Consulate and they got me out of the country. Look, I will tell you the rest of the story after you are done in here." Jack and Thor left the room as Tess began to riffle through her clothes.

As fascinating as the background story was, Tess knew she had to attempt to escape; she really could not wait around to hear the rest. She would have to somehow lock up Thor and make a break for it during the daylight hours. With this goal in mind, she quickly showered, dressed in sweats and put on her running shoes. Jack was brilliant and observant, she would need to get the upper hand the moment she went into the living room.

"All right, let the interrogation begin." Tess settled herself into an overstuffed armchair by the front door feigning a relaxed posture. "I assume all of the rooms in the house are bugged."

"All but the bathrooms and bedrooms." Jack sat down on the L-shaped couch facing her. "Let's go back to Sara and the train explosion. By the way, I have to compliment you on your Oscar winning performance, between the rolling eyes, slurred speech and constant tangents, I thought you were very convincing, I especially enjoyed the Alfred Nobel detour."

"Why thank you sir, once a historian always a historian. Listen Jack, you have information I want and I have information you need. Let's make a pact to be honest with each other from now on and see where that leads us." Tess leaned forward and held out her hand, which Jack took, made a slight bow over and kissed.

"I'll take that as a 'Yes', first I am going to let Thor out for a few minutes." Tess whistled for Thor, walked with him to the back door and locked him in on the porch. She quickly closed the door and sat back down so Jack would not feel the need to investigate whether Thor had actually gone outside. "As you have already told me, you know that the Suffragettes in the U. K. were waging a more violent campaign than the Suffragists in the U. S."

Tess began to play her Scheherazade role. "Even though we trace our first women's rights movement back to 1848, the U. K. goes back even further. The first women's suffrage bill was presented to the House of Commons in 1832; it was introduced again in 1867 by John Stuart Mill . . ." Tess looked up as Jack began to speak.

"John Stuart Mill the English philosopher and economist?" Jack leaned forward, resting his flannel clad arms on his legs.

"Right, one in the same, he and his wife Harriet Taylor Mill were considered to be the leading feminists of the nineteenth century. Mill was a great friend of Emmeline Pankhurst's family, so you can see that the Pankhurst's involvement with the suffrage movement was multi-generational." Tess leaned back in her chair to check and see if Thor was visible on the porch.

"The reason that I am telling you this is because I don't want you to get the impression that the Suffragettes were a crazy bunch of terrorists. In fact, several prominent families were involved in the movement. Octavia Wilberforce, the great-granddaughter of William Wilberforce was a member of the WSPU." Tess looked to Jack to see if he recognized the name.

"William Wilberforce, the MP who fought for the abolition of the slave trade?" Jack was clearly impressed with the noble lineage of the movement.

"Yes, a keen interest in social reform runs in the Wilberforce family. Things began to heat up in 1903 with the founding of the WSPU and their decision to use, 'Deeds, Not Words', as their motto. From 1905-1910 more militant activities took place, the Suffragettes held huge rallies, were arrested, beaten and then force fed when they went on hunger-strikes. Emmeline believed that her sister Mary Clarke

died from the damage she sustained while being force fed."
Tess looked for understanding in Jack's eyes as he spoke.

"All of this pain, torture and even death, just for the right
to vote, a right that women should have always had." Jack
shook his head.

"I know it's hard to fathom in the 21st Century. Anyway,
Sara joined up just as the intense arson and bombing
campaign began. In February of 1913, David Lloyd George's
house, Pinfold Manor, was bombed. This is when he was still
Chancellor of the Exchequer, before he became Prime
Minister. Sara told my grandmother that she and her friend
Emily Wilding Davison planted the bomb . . ." Jack leaned
forward.

"Wait, I know that name, wasn't she the woman who
threw herself in front of King George V's horse at the Epsom
Derby?"

"Well that is one of the versions; Sara explained that
Emily had attempted to attach a 'Votes for Women' banner
onto Anmer, the king's horse as it reached the finish line. The
fact that Davison had purchased a return railway ticket and
she had planned to meet Sara at a Suffragette dance that
night supports Sara's story." Tess glanced out the back
windows of the house.

"But Anmer slammed into her and killed her." Jack looked sickened at the thought of what a massive racehorse, running at full speed, could do to a woman's body.

"Yes, she was crushed into the track and died of internal injuries four days later. I have seen the original Pathe News footage of Davison being run over, it is appalling; I think that is when Sara lost it. According to my grandmother, Sara vowed to make King George V pay. She somehow discovered that he had commissioned a special train, supposedly filled with priceless antiques, that was due to arrive in London on June 10th." Tess stopped as Jack stood up and began to pace in front of her.

"So that was the train Nathan's grandfather was secretly traveling on. But why? Why would a Russian man, carrying a briefcase with the largest ruby in the world, be on that train?"

"Good question, obviously Nathan and the U. S. government does not know who had possession of the Flame in 1913. Think about it Jack, who had the most power, influence and astounding wealth in Russia at the time." Tess was relieved to see Jack sit back down on the couch, he had been standing in her flight path.

"Oh, hell, Czar Nicholas II, or more probably his wife Alexandra, but why would she send the Flame to England?"

Jack's expressive brown eyes rested on Tess' face as she leaned forward to provide the last piece of the puzzle.

"Czarina Alexandra's mother was Princess Alice, Queen Victoria's daughter; that made King George V her cousin. Alexandra was heavily influenced by that madman Rasputin, and from what we have learned, he had some sort of premonition that the family would 'Fall from grace', as he put it. He convinced Alexandra to begin sending some of her jewels to her family in England for safe keeping." Tess carefully watched Jack as he began to process this new information. She wondered what their minders were doing at that moment. It amused her to think of agents scurrying around trying to confirm the details of her story.

So far, she was keeping her part of the bargain, by providing the U. S. government with the Russian connection to the Flame it would buy her time. She still had to find out the specifics of the Brazilian, Indian and Portuguese claim.

"It seems improbable that Rasputin knew about the Bolshevik Revolution, after all, that happened in 1917 and Sara blew up the train in 1913. Of course, he could have been making an educated guess, based upon the fact that Russia was basically a feudal society. Millions of peasants toiling under repressive conditions; a vast urban poor and arrogant nobility, it sounds like the makings of a revolution to me. In fact, the conditions are eerily similar to King Louis XVI in France, and we know what happened there." Jack seemed poised to get up but Tess' inquiry stopped him.

"Now you and your listeners know all of the background that we have on the Flame. It's time to share your info, as a gesture of good faith." Tess needed to find out more about the Brazilian and Portuguese connections. The ruby was called the Flame of Brazil, so obviously it had, at one time, been associated with that country. The Sisterhood had never been able to trace the stone's provenance beyond Czarina Alexandra.

If Tess could get Jack to open up about Brazil and Portugal, then the Sisterhood would be able to take measures to protect itself against their enquiries. If what Jack said was true, and she really didn't have any reason to doubt it, then Russian operatives were in the field at this moment. If the Russians were sending out agents, then it stood to reason that the U.K., Brazil and Portugal would follow suit. Aside from all of those countries, what did India have to do with all of this? God, what an unholy mess, Tess had to get the Flame and get rid of it.

"That seems like a fair request, it is quite simple. The Flame of Brazil is not really from Brazil; the stone was originally called the Blood of India. I discovered the ruby's background while living in Mumbai. Remember I told you that I had been doing research on the Taj Mahal?" Jack looked to Tess as she bobbed her head.

"Right, well I found an obscure reference to, the Blood of India, and I began to follow that lead. I combed through original documents that had not seen the light of day in centuries. The librarians at the university knew me by reputation and they trusted me. I promised to catalogue and scan everything I came across. Like all libraries around the world, they have too many documents and not enough people." As Jack paused Tess realized that he was a magnificent specimen, she was going to miss him.

She had never really believed in indiscriminate coupling, no one-night stands for her, but she was as susceptible as any woman to Jack's smoky/spicy scent and athletic build.

"Hey, are you in there?" Jack was waving his hand in front of her face. "Anyone home?"

"Oh, sorry Jack, it's not that I'm not interested; it's just a lot to take in." She could hardly admit that he had interrupted her in the middle of imagining the two of them naked and rolling around on his crazy old bed. "Please continue; it is really the Blood of India."

"The Taj Mahal is the mausoleum where Mumtaz Mahal is entombed; she was the wife of Shan Jahan, the ruler of India. Mahal was a Persian princess that was married to Jahan, and according to my research, the light of his life. When she died giving birth to their fourteenth child, he was inconsolable. In 1653 he entombed his beloved Mumtaz and the Blood Of India in the Taj Mahal." Jack ran his eyes up and down her body; then continued.

"I can imagine how Jahan felt . . ." Jack cleared his throat and began again, "the Blood of India is reported to have weighed anywhere from nine to twelve pounds, making it the largest uncut ruby in the world, then and now. I assume that the Blood's estimated worth would be in the tens of millions today. Now do you see why I want you to give it to us? This secret has lain dormant for over one hundred years. The Sisterhood's time is up, everyone knows."

Tess arose from the chair and moved toward the front door feigning a contemplative pose. She had to find out the Brazilian/Portuguese history and then she would run. Over a decade of training had prepared her for moments such as this. She had to be more cunning, faster and more agile than her pursuer; Jack was about to be tested.

"Thanks Jack, I do appreciate your honesty. Now I understand the Indian government's claim. It would seem that the Indian people are the rightful owners of the Flame or Blood, whatever you call it. To be perfectly honest I would like to get rid of the thing. Because we have been the Keepers for four generations, our family has been on constant alert. The possibility of giving up that responsibility is very attractive." Tess paused as if she were considering her options. In reality she would never give up the location of the Flame.

"I was wondering why you called yourself Keeper Three back at the cabin? If it is four generations, why are you Keeper Three?" Jack followed her movements with his eyes.

"It's simple really, a man can't be a Keeper. The line goes from Sara to my grandma Ruth, then my dad was skipped, and it fell to me. Sara was Keeper One, grandma was Keeper Two, until I turned sixteen and I became Keeper Three. My dad never knew anything about the Sisterhood." Tess moved incrementally closer to the front door. "Could you please explain to me how the Blood ended up in Brazil?"

"Well, in a nutshell; the Portuguese explorer Vasco da Gama opened up the oceanic trade routes to India in the late fifteenth/early sixteenth centuries. From the information that I unearthed, the Blood of India went missing from the Taj Mahal during the Emperor Aurangzeb's reign; Aurangzeb was Shan Jahan and Mumtaz Mahal's son. I found an obscure reference to, 'the desecration of the royal tomb of the sacred mother,' which I deduced was Mahal's tomb." Jack paused to see if Tess was following his explanation. She nodded.

"da Gama died in 1525 and Aurangzeb ruled from 1658-1707; which means that da Gama himself did not steal the Blood. As far as I can make out, a group of Portuguese traders somehow discovered the location of the Blood, broke into the Taj Mahal and took it. I followed the Blood's trail to Portugal and talked my way into the National Archives. From the information that I found there, I discovered that the Braganza family, which was the royal household of Portugal, had somehow acquired the Blood." Jack stopped his narrative as Tess leaned against the front door. She motioned for him to continue.

"In 1807 the Braganza family fled to Rio de Janeiro, Brazil because the Napoleonic Wars were ravaging Europe. I assume they took everything of value that they had. According to the National Archives, in 1821 the bulk of the royal family returned to Portugal, however, Prince Pedro chose to stay. In 1822 he declared Brazil to be a constitutional monarchy. At that time the Blood of India, now renamed the Flame of Brazil, was placed on display in the National Palace." Jack leaned back into the couch.

"Wow, that was quite a 'nutshell,' I can tell you that the Sisterhood has never been able to figure out how the Flame made its way from Brazil into the hands of the Russian royal family." Tess shifted her weight forward ever so slightly.

"So far, I have not been able to find that particular link. What the U.S. government does know is that in the months leading up to WWI, Nathan's grandfather was accidentally killed in a train explosion caused by Sara. Russian, British and American officials believe that Sara found the Blood, fled Great Britain to avoid prosecution, and made her way to the U.S. Will you at least confirm that?" Jack looked to Tess.

"I will. You are correct. Sara did plant the bomb, only to blow up antiques, and she did inadvertently kill Nathan's grandfather. She found the Flame, let's just call it the Blood, and jumped on the next ship out of the U.K. Sara befriended the American Suffragists and helped them with their cause. I will need to contact the Sisterhood and give them all of this info. Then we can discuss handing over the Blood to the Indian authorities. Does that sound reasonable?" Tess watched as Jack visibly relaxed. That was the moment she had been waiting for. She quickly threw the door open and sprinted across the drive.

CHAPTER EIGHT

"What the hell do you mean by coming in here and telling me how to do my job?" Sheriff Mike was pacing back and forth in front of a clearly intimidated young man in a dark suit and tie. Edward, Mason and Deb squirmed in their respective seats. "I don't know what the FBI has to do with this case but I am not just going to turn everything over to you!"

"Sheriff, with all due respect, please don't shoot the messenger. I only know what my superiors in D.C. tell me. The dead man was part of a local drug ring, we believe he was killed by his fellow dealers, your missing criminal has been found and arrested, the two students were offered jobs with a computer company in California and Dr. Rankin is helping us with our investigation." With that, Agent Howard offered his hand to Mike. "Thank you for your time, I better be going, I have to catch the next plane to D.C."

"Not so fast, Slick. I don't believe one word that has come out of your mouth since you got here. Your minders obviously thought that I would go easy on a new recruit; they were wrong. Now you are going to sit here until I get some answers or . . ." Mike paused as his cell phone rang. He grabbed it off his desk, motioned for the FBI agent to stay put and disappeared down the hall. Agent Howard took the opportunity to race out the front door, jump into a black SUV and drive away.

Edward and Mason popped up and began to yell as Deb silently made her packing list. Even though it was autumn in Wyoming, it would be late spring in New Zealand. She had been waiting for the final confirmation of her worst fears; the appearance of the FBI agent was it. Tess was in some sort of danger. Deb didn't know the specifics; she didn't need to. This morning she had gone to the bank, opened up the safety deposit box and taken out the contents.

Deb blocked out Edward's and Mason's explanations to her dad while she thought back to the day that Tess had given her the key to the safety deposit box. It had been the most horrific summer of their lives. They had just turned sixteen and were still reeling from the fact that Tess' parents had died in April. Nana and Papa, Tess' grandparents, decided to take Tess to Japan for the summer. They felt the extreme change of scenery would be just what she needed.

Deb never knew the exact story, however, Tess had come home, literally, in pieces. Nana and Papa had told everyone that Tess had been in a car accident; Deb had never believed that. Tess had a broken arm, broken pelvis, two broken legs and various head injuries. When she had fully recovered she gave Deb the key to a safety deposit box and made her promise that if she ever disappeared Deb would open the box.

At the time Deb had been confused and frightened, but she had kept her word, however, as the years passed Tess had never given her a moment of worry. Until yesterday Deb hadn't considered the possibility that she might ever have to use the key. Tess had continued to travel with Nana and Papa every summer and she had always come back healthy and fit. In fact, Tess had returned each time stronger and more self-assured. The only lingering affect of her injuries seemed to be an aversion to boys.

Try as she might, Deb could not ease the apprehension Tess felt concerning the scars on her body. It was a sad fact that Tess was so self-conscious she had only one date in high school, the Senior Prom with Edward's friend Ken. Over time Tess had slowly developed the ability to relate to males although she had never been in a serious relationship.

Now she was missing. Deb had to agree with her dad, she didn't believe a word that Agent Howard had uttered. For some inexplicable reason the FBI was holding Tess against her will or was covering up information regarding Tess' whereabouts. Deb had contacted Tess' department chair at the university and he told her Agent Howard had requested that all of Tess' classes be switched to online courses.

The university had reluctantly agreed to the FBI's demands. Deb now understood that Tess was not expected to be back to work until the Spring semester began the first of February. Deb slowly removed her cell phone and gun from their respective clips on her belt and locked them in her desk.

"Dad I think you need to contact your old army buddy at the CIA and see if he can help us." Deb walked up to her dad and fixed his ever-askew tie. She fought back tears as she considered the danger she might be walking into.

"You're right honey, I don't know why I didn't think of Stan before. I'm gonna call him right now. Edward, get on over to the university and talk to everyone in the history department; I also want you to search Tess' office. Mason, go out to Tess' ranch and see if Redhawk or any of the kids from the reservation have heard from her. I want you to go over her house with a fine-tooth comb." Mike absentmindedly patted Deb on the head and walked into the conference room.

"Babydoll, you need to get right now before they notice how strange you been acting." Miz Robinson wrapped her arms around Deb and kissed her forehead.

"Wait ma'am, how do you know I'm planning on leaving?" Deb looked up at her mother-in-law in wonder.

"Sweetpea, I know a whole lotta things that you don't. Just trust in yourself and Tess. Do exactly what the letter says and you gonna be all right. Now take this . . ." Miz Robinson removed a fine silver chain from her pocket and placed it around Deb's neck, at the end of the chain hung a delicate silver cross with a rose wrapped around it, "and hightail it outta here."

Deb kissed her on the cheek, checked to see if her father was out of sight and raced for the door. She jumped into her truck and quickly drove home. Deb and Edward lived on a small, ten-acre, spread just outside the Jameson city limits. The house and land had been a wedding present from her parents. Deb thanked her lucky stars that her mother had lived to see her only child married. Her mom had died of breast cancer two months after the wedding.

Five years had passed and her father had never moved on; although lately Deb had noticed her father looking at Miz Robinson when he didn't think anyone was paying attention. Maybe there was something he wasn't telling her. She didn't have time to consider the ramifications of that possible relationship.

She looked at the various pictures hanging on the living room wall. There were dozens of shots of two little girls with their arms wrapped around each other. Their heads tilted together. She had to go; she had to help Tess. They were sisters.

Deb went into the master bedroom and began to pack. She looked at the contents of the safety deposit box one last time. The box had held a letter addressed to her, a passport with her face but a different name and five thousand dollars in cash as well as five thousand pounds of currency from New Zealand. Deb reread the letter for the tenth time.

Dear Deb,

If you are reading this letter something has happened to me. I can't give you very much information; please just trust me. I need you to use the money to fly to Los Angeles under your real name; then purchase a ticket to Auckland, New Zealand under the name on the passport.

When you arrive in Auckland fly to Queenstown and register at The Dairy Private Luxury Hotel. You will be contacted by my organization upon your arrival. You are the best friend I have ever had and I know that we will make it through whatever peril we are now facing. Please don't tell anyone where you are going; my life may depend upon it.

All my love,

Tess

Deb had made her plane reservation to L.A., but she had not used her computer to check any more information, better not to leave any trail. She didn't know if she would need a visa to enter New Zealand, she figured she would deal with the ticket and anything else at L.A. International. She finished her packing, changed into Levi's and a tee shirt, placed the money, letter and passport into her purse and sat down to write the most difficult letter of her life.

Try as she might, there would be no way to explain to Edward what she was doing. She didn't even really understand what was going on. She had no idea what Tess meant by, "Her organization", Tess worked at the university, she didn't have an organization. Deb was absolutely certain of two things: Tess was in trouble and she had to help.

She finished the letter, placed it on their bed and locked the door behind her. As she drove out of town she put all thoughts of Edward, her dad and Jameson out of her mind. There was just one nagging question. What did her mother-in-law have to do with all of this?

CHAPTER NINE

Tess could hear the frenzied barking of Thor as she raced across the driveway, down the road and through the trees toward Sixteenmile River. When she entered the forest she sensed someone moving very rapidly behind her. Jack would not bother to call after her. He would be quick and silent.

As noiselessly as possible she veered left toward the river. If she could just make it to the water she would be able to acclimate herself. Tess had once spent an entire summer in the Black Forest in Germany on an orienteering course. Niels, her six-foot six Dutch guide, had been brutally effective with his training. Tess had learned how to survive in the wild for weeks.

All of her extensive, and let's face it, expensive, training was not needed now. She just had to keep Jack out of the house for a few minutes so that the Sisterhood could slip in and plant their listening devices. The techs were extremely efficient; she assumed it would not take them more than ten minutes.

Her plan was twofold, she wanted the bugs planted and she needed Jack to think that she was trying to escape. Jack was a brilliant man; he would not be fooled by her seemingly cooperative behavior for very long. Now she would give him what he had been suspiciously waiting for. She found herself in a heavily wooded section as she made her way south towards the river.

Visions of Bigfoot sprang to mind when she heard a slight rustling in a thicket directly in front of her. She froze in alarm as a harmless doe tentatively stepped out of the brush and moved toward her. Tess took a moment to listen for Jack. Nothing. She had to hand it to him, he must have been fairly close, but she could not detect any movement.

She quietly made her way to the riverbank; still no sign of Jack. As she inched along the tree line she suddenly heard the snap of a branch. Yes! She had him now; or he had her. It really didn't matter.

By the time she graciously surrendered and they walked back to the house all of the devices would be in place. Tess moved deeper into the ancient forest, this time making sure that her footfalls could be easily heard.

She came upon a enormous tree with low-hanging branches and she briefly considered climbing up and waiting for Jack. Better not; no need to mock him. A loud thump followed by a snort literally stopped her in her tracks.

She desperately searched the trees for any sign of a wild boar, a recent arrival to Montana, or worse a wolf. Since the restrictions on the hunting of wolves had been in place the packs had come roaring back with a vengeance.

A strange sniffing broke into her terrified thoughts. She had been trying to remember everything she knew about wolves and how to fight off an attack. Oh, what she would give for her precious gun about now. The wild boars had huge tusks that would be lethal, but the wolves were extraordinary hunters and they traveled in packs.

Slowly, silently, she moved toward a small clearing as a massive shadow crossed her path. She spun around just in time to confront one of the most terrifying predators in the world, a Grizzly bear. Grizzly bears come in all colors; this one had gray streaks. The certain way to tell a Grizzly from any other large bear was the distinctive hump above the shoulders. This bear was roughly the size of a bulldozer.

The menacing monster stopped within twenty feet of Tess as he raised his head and shook it from side to side. He seemed to be catching a scent or listening for movement. Tess froze. She knew that Grizzlies went into hibernation in late November and this was their peak hunting time as they stored up their fat reserves for the winter.

The bear swung around to face her and began to sniff the air. Her brain went into over-drive as she desperately tried to remember how to survive an encounter with one of these beasts. Only one thought burst through her terror-numbed mind; Night of the Grizzlies.

In the early morning hours of August the 13th 1967, two groups of campers, miles apart, were set upon by Grizzlies in Glacier National Park, the Grizzlies mauled several of the campers and killed a woman at each site. Every Montanan knew the horrifying story of that tragic night; the main reason some of the campers survived was because they had the presence of mind to get up into the farthest branches of a nearby tree. Grizzlies could climb trees, however, they were so large they could not go out on the smaller limbs.

Tess carefully pivoted and began to gingerly move toward the huge tree with the low branches as the bear watched her progress. Step by step the Grizzly intently observed her cautious movements until she reached the base of the tree. As Tess slowly reached for the nearest branch the bear exploded with a deafening roar; she almost lost her balance as the earth shook from the violent pounding of the bear's massive paws. She had never seen such a huge animal move so fast. The Grizzly was upon her before she could even register that it had moved.

She grabbed the branch and swung up into the tree, climbing for all she was worth. As she scrambled higher and higher the bear kept pace with her. Each time she moved farther up the surprisingly nimble Grizzly's razor sharp claws swiped within inches of her feet. On and on she climbed trying to keep her balance as the tree shuddered from the force of the bear. One word managed to wrench itself from her terror stricken throat.

"Jack!" She screamed as the bear began to roar in what she assumed was frustration.

"Jack! Jack! Jack! Help me! Help!" Tess' cries pierced the forest as the bear's furious growls reverberated through the tree. Tess' muscles were shaking from the strain and sweat was pouring down her back as she desperately struggled up branch by branch. The Grizzly continued its ear-shattering roars in between violent grunts. Tess never looked back or broke her stride as she clawed her way up. She was relived to see that the branches were getting smaller and more delicate the farther she went.

While she continued her mad rush upwards she, she sensed the bear's pace slowing. She heard grunts as the lower branches began to crash under the Grizzly's weight.

Just as she swung up onto a smaller branch the bear made one last desperate lunge for her ankle and connected. Searing pain tore through her leg as she screamed in agony. The bear took full advantage of her momentary pause to shift its weight and attempt another swipe as a series of shots echoed through the forest.

Tess felt a hot gush of blood spatter as the Grizzly bellowed and dropped to the ground. She could not see the injured bear through the canopy, but sounds of thrashing around assured her it was still alive. Several more shots were fired in succession and then the only sound that could be heard was the birdcalls.

"Tess, my God! Are you okay!" Jack called up into the thick green mass.

"Jack, thank heaven." Tess burst into sobs as she attempted to dislodge herself from her perch. "Jack, my legs seemed to have given out on me. Could you please help me?"

"Don't move, I'm coming, are you hurt, did I hit you?" Jack's head popped through a clearing in the branches, as Tess shifted her weight off her injured leg.

"No, don't worry, you didn't shoot me. The Grizzly managed to get a last hit before he fell. My shoe saved my foot, but my leg looks pretty bad." Tess managed a painful smile as Jack came into view.

"Okay, don't worry everything will be fine. I'm here and I got ya. Just try to turn around and climb down into my arms." Jack wrapped his arms around Tess and gave her a rib-cracking squeeze. "There now, I will support you as you come down, don't worry about your leg, we will take care of it when we get back to the house."

With Jack's help Tess managed to reach the ground within minutes. It seemed odd that it only took a short time to descend considering the fact that the upward climb felt like an eternity. Tess dropped to the ground as Jack tore open her pant leg and looked at the wound. There were several angry looking rips in her skin that were oozing blood.

"Yikes, that's going to leave a mark." Tess managed to give Jack a brave grin.

"Tess you are the most infuriating woman I have ever met. You were almost killed by one of the most dangerous predators on earth and you are cracking jokes. Wait! You are covered in blood! Where else are you hurt?" Jack began to run his hands all over Tess.

"Stop mauling me! That's from the Grizzly not me!" Tess shoved Jack away as she attempted to stand. The effort was wasted; she keeled over and landed directly on top of the dead bear. "Oh my God! That is so gross!" Tess rolled off the bear and struggled to her knees.

"Tess we have to get out of here. Grizzlies are like sharks; they can smell blood from unbelievable distances. This place could be crawling with bears any minute. Jump in the river and try to wash off as much blood as possible and then let's get out of here. Come on we won't have much time." Jack helped Tess regain her feet and walked her to the river's edge. Tess submerged herself in the water and then pulled off her blood soaked socks, shoes and pants. Jack tore a ribbon of material from his shirt, wrapped her ankle and hoisted her on his back.

"Here take this . . ." Jack handed her his shotgun "and hang on tight." Jack took off through the forest at a brisk pace as Tess tried to hold the gun and cling to him. Several times they heard the sounds of something large crashing through the trees, however, nothing seemed to be headed their way.

After what seemed like an eternity, the house came into view. Jack sprinted the last few steps, walked through the open door and gently placed Tess on the couch. "Just rest here, I'm going to let Thor out for a minute and then we will batten down the hatches."

Jack walked to the back porch where Thor was attempting to claw his way into her. Thor leapt up and landed directly on her wound. As Tess let out a moan, Jack grabbed Thor and pulled him outside. They returned in a matter of seconds. This time Thor walked over and dropped down on the rug at her feet.

"Hey, anyone who might be listening . . ." Jack spoke to the open air of the living room, "you need to know that I killed a Grizzly and I would bet that this section of the forest will become a hot zone any minute. I suggest you take the necessary precautions." With that announcement, Jack walked toward the front door.

Tess watched in amazement as Jack opened a wooden box on the wall and began to flip switches. Suddenly there was a loud reverberation throughout the house as thick metal panels rolled out of the walls in front of all the doors and windows. Jack had not been exaggerating; as of that moment the log home was an impenetrable fortress. No bear, Grizzly or not, could smash its way through the log walls and all of the other entrances were covered on the outside by what looked to be heavy steel.

"Tess let me get you some water and something for the pain while I clean up your leg." Jack walked into the kitchen and came back with his supplies. He began to wash the wound while Tess tossed the pill into her mouth and gulped down the entire glass.

"Jack, I don't know what to say; I am so sorry. Because of my stupid stunt you might have been hurt and then you were forced to kill that amazing animal." Now that she was no longer in danger Tess could appreciate the wild beauty of the Grizzly. She was ashamed that she had caused the death of such a magnificent specimen. Granted, the bear had been trying to eat her, however, it was not at fault for pursuing its natural circle of life.

"Don't dwell on that now. I'm just about finished here. You won't need stitches, but I imagine you will have a reminder of your encounter for the rest of your life." Jack wrapped a bandage around her ankle and taped off the end. "Now you need to get into some fresh clothes and rest. You've had quite a scare and you might be feeling the shock of your adventure any moment." As Jack uttered his last word, Thor jumped up and raced for the door with a raucous bark.

"Oh no, here they come." Jack's voice trailed off as a terrifying wrenching sound echoed through the house.

"My God Jack! What is that?!!" Tess tried to stand, but the minute she put pressure on her ankle a hot branding iron of pain shot up her leg. She dropped back on the couch and curled into the corner, pulling a blanket up to her shoulders. Thor raced from room to room growling and barking.

"We have company. I believe the sound we are hearing . . ." Jack was interrupted by a series of roars that answered Thor's barks. Tess strained to remember information about bears and dogs being natural enemies. The fact that Thor was inside seemed to enrage the bear even more; in fact, it almost sounded as if there were a couple of bears outside, " . . . is the porch being ripped to shreds." Jack got up, reloaded his shotgun and handed it to her. "I assume you know how to use one of these."

"Yes Jack, I can handle it." Tess watched Jack open a closet and pulled out a handgun and a rifle. "What do you want me to do?" Tess rearranged herself to face the front door.

"Stay where you are; if anything comes through that door shoot first and hang the consequences. I'm going to check every room in the house to make sure all of the steel sheets are in place. Keep Thor by you." With that, Jack disappeared upstairs.

Thor continued to race back and forth between the front and back doors as Tess cringed every time a wrenching sound emanated from, what she assumed to be the destroyed back porch. She hoped that her retrieval team had placed the bugs and heard Jack's warning to his people before the protective plates had come down. She knew that there would be some sort of interference with the Sisterhood's and the government's surveillance now that the windows and doors were sealed off.

A thundering crash caused the front door to shake as Thor launched himself against it, tearing at it with his paws and teeth. The sound of the dog seemed to enrage the bear as it beat a continuous cacophony of sledgehammer like blows against the, hopefully, un-wielding steel. Jack came down the stairs and began to make a fire.

"I don't know if this will work, but I hope the smell of the smoke will throw them off the scent of blood. At least it's worth a try. I raised one of the protective plates on a window upstairs and it looks as if we have two Grizzlies attempting to get into the house. The back porch is completely gone and they tried to get into the garbage but the anti-bear openings foiled their plans." Jack lit the fire and closed the glass screen as Thor jumped up on the couch with Tess.

If they hadn't been in mortal danger, the room would have had a nice ambiance. Jack settled himself and his weapons on the couch next to Thor. "The pounding has stopped, maybe the smoke is confusing them. Either way, those sheets won't go up until morning. Hey, Tess are you okay? You look a little green." Jack put down his guns and moved toward her.

"I'm feeling kinda funky; what was that pill you gave me?" Tess stretched out on the couch as Jack kneeled on the floor beside her.

"Don't worry, I wouldn't give you anything that will hurt you. You are going to sleep for a bit and hopefully feel better in the morning." Jack reached up and began to gently stroke her hair.

"Jack, if you don't stop drugging me I'm going to kick your . . ." With that useless threat hanging in the air; Tess drifted off to sleep.

CHAPTER TEN

Tess was in agony. As she gently shifted her weight, the rock hard mattress bit into her bruises. Yesterday's training had been particularly brutal. Robert and Reem had put Tess and her new friend Liz Montalvo through the most difficult training session of the summer. The dojo had been sweltering, the water had been scarce and the bamboo training sticks had managed to hit the two girls in every conceivable part of their bodies. Not for the first time that summer, Tess contemplated giving up.

The pain over the loss of her parents was a searing wound. Every morning she woke up listening for their familiar treads. Every morning she relived the horror of their deaths. Every morning she hoped that the last few months had all been a horrid dream. Finally, she gathered her courage, got out of bed and sent a silent prayer to her parents, vowing to carry on the family legacy and make them proud.

So this was her destiny. She was training to be The Keeper. The last of a line, begun by her great-grandmother Sara, continued on through her grandmother Ruth (who had married her grandfather Chester), skipped over in the case of her father, which finally led to her. When Nana and Papa had explained, to the still reeling Tess, the family legacy, she had stared dumbfounded. The entire implausible story had sounded like something out of a novel.

Militant Suffragettes, bombs, murder and a jewel heist didn't quite jive with the family history Tess knew. Growing up she had been told that the Rankin family had lived on their bison ranch in Wyoming for almost two hundred years. The only family connection to a famous woman was the fact that her great-grandfather Clement had been related to Jeannette Rankin, the first woman elected to the U. S. Congress.

Tess shook Liz awake and joined her for a quick granola bar as they made their way to the training dojo. The compound was located in the mountains near the small village of Arashiyama, Japan. Tess looked down through the dense bamboo groves, past the wooden Togetsu-kyo, (Moon-Crossing Bridge) out to the Oi River.

The lush green fields, forests and groves looked deceptively cool. Week after week as Tess and Liz worked their way through various types of martial arts training, Arashiyama began to heat up. By the end of July it was a pleasure to be in the mountains. Their closest neighbor was the monkey park, from which emanated a constant screech.

They began their training at 6:00 a.m., Monday through Saturday, in a large wooden structure with mats on the floor and every conceivable weapon on the walls. They practiced until noon and then were joined by Nana and Papa for lunch. Afternoon instruction continued until 6:00 p.m., when they had dinner. Liz's parents were back home in New York so she was folded into the Rankin family unit; Liz had been placed in the program by her mother, who was the New York City representative for the Sisterhood.

This morning they were to begin their advanced protective techniques, or as Liz had dubbed it, Killing School. Little did they know that by the end of the day, they would literally, be fighting for their lives. Reem began working with Liz. At "five feet nothing", as her brother called her, Reem was a safer match for the petit, although voluptuous, Liz. Liz's family was originally from Puerto Rico and her long glossy black hair, bronzed skin and pitch perfect Spanish reflected her Latina heritage. Robert moved Tess across the room to give each pair plenty of space.

As Reem was little, Robert was large. Although they shared dark southern Italian features, Robert towered over everyone at the dojo, with a booming voice that emanated from his barrel chest. The intense hand-to-hand combat progressed clumsily at first until each of the girls began to anticipate moves and strikes.

Sweat poured down their tee shirt and shorts clad bodies. The training session did not end until both girls ran outside and threw up. That seemed to be the signal that Robert and Reem had waited for.

After a lunch of broth, water and bread the girls returned for their regular combined session with the master of the dojo, Mr. Hagiwara. The girls loved their master. He was everything they had imagined when they arrived in June. He was endlessly patient, kind, brilliant and funny. To be sure, he was an exacting taskmaster, however, he never belittled or humiliated them.

As much as the girls looked forward to working with Mr. Hagiwara, they loathed his occasional substitute. A brute of a man named Dalton who had an accent that Tess could never quite place. Dalton routinely used excessive force and in one instance had used the cover of training to grope both Tess and Liz.

The girls had reported the incident to Robert and Reem. Since that day Dalton had backed off. Tess assumed Robert had applied considerable force to any discussion.

After dinner with Nana and Papa, the girls returned to their room for a well-deserved rest. They were not alarmed when the room phone ran and it was the porter telling them to return to the dojo. Mr. Hagiwara often would call them for additional training in the cooler hours of the late evening. The girls changed into tank tops and shorts and headed down the path. Partway, Tess realized that she had forgotten her training gloves and she turned back to the room as Liz carried on.

It took her a few minutes to locate them; however, when she did she raced for the dojo out of respect for her master. As she slipped through the door, she was struck by the quiet. Only one small light cast a yellow glow across a far corner of the room. She turned to head out thinking that the session had been canceled, when she heard a slight scrape that sounded as if a chair was moving across the wooden floor.

In a moment that would haunt her for the rest of her life, she made the decision to investigate the sound. She silently walked across the floor mats and peered around the movable wall. A jolt of terror struck her as she stared in horror at the sight of Liz bound, gagged and tied to a chair. Tess moved toward Liz as her friend began to frantically scream, thrash around and bite at the gag. Liz's eyes widened as Tess felt a massive hand cover her mouth.

"Hello puppet, so glad you could join us." Dalton's odious voice whispered into her ear. Struggle as she may; Tess could not keep him from shoving a ball into her mouth and fixing it with a buckle gag. "Now since your little friend is safely trussed up, I think I will start with you." A backhand across her face sent Tess flying onto the mat. Through the ringing in her ears Tess could hear Liz banging the chair into the floor.

"Knock around all you want, no one can hear you." Dalton sneered as he advanced across the mats toward a shaken Tess. She knew what he said was heartbreakingly true. The dojo was down the hill from the rest of the buildings in the most isolated section of the complex.

She was no match for his strength or skill. Tess realized that he meant to beat her, rape her and probably kill her, then start in on Liz. Even with a decade of training she still would not be able to survive this night without a weapon.

"Okay, I should warn you that I like to play with my food." Dalton picked up Tess and threw her into the wall several times before dropping her back on the mat.

Searing pain sent shock waves through her body as Tess fought to keep from passing out. She had time to observe Liz's frantic struggles as Dalton raised his boot-clad foot and stomped it down on her arm. Mind-numbing agony engulfed her as she heard a loud crack and saw a section of broken bone slice through her skin.

"So princess, have I taught you nothing. You disappoint me. All summer long we have been training you, now you find yourself in real world conditions and you don't even put up a fight." Dalton continued his incessant mocking but Tess had tuned him out. She fixated on one simple word: fight. She was down, but she would fight. She was in excruciating pain, but she would fight. Against all odds, she would fight.

Tess rolled across the floor and stood shakily on her feet. She looked past Dalton and locked eyes with Liz. Liz nodded her head and began to inch her hands towards the bindings and kick the legs of the chair. Tess' only hope was to try and stall Dalton long enough for Liz to get free and then they both could take him. She surveyed the weapon-covered walls as she backed toward the one closest to her.

Dalton leisurely strolled across the mats. "Oh wonderful, this is more like it. Now let's see what you are made of." He rushed headlong at Tess as she quickly side-stepped him and ran toward the wall. "Not so fast, sweet cheeks." A lighting fast kick to the back of her knee dropped Tess. She vaguely understood that the odd angle of her leg meant it was broken.

Using her good arm and leg she dragged her near-inert body toward the wall. When Dalton had thrown her into it, one of the knives had broken loose and now lay on the floor. If she could just get it before he realized what had happened she might have a slim chance.

Tess looked over her shoulder at the menacing figure as he advanced. She lunged for the knife at the same time Dalton raised his boot and slammed it into her back. A hideous crunching sound reverberated through the dojo.

Enveloped in a tunnel of pain, Tess barely registered Dalton delivering another deadly blow to her functioning leg. She was helpless, immobile, but strangely focused. Within her remaining, non-injured hand she held the knife. Dalton chuckled as he methodically pulled her shorts off of her inert body and flipped her on her back.

"I have been waiting all summer to do this, watching and planning for just the right moment. My favorite pastime is raping virgins; two in one night has always been a fantasy of mine. Let's get this party started." Dalton stepped out of his pants as Liz loomed up behind him and thrust a dagger into the back of his neck. He screamed in agony and dropped to the ground as Tess sliced her knife across his jugular vein. He bled out in minutes.

Liz rushed to Tess' side, removed the gag and tried to gather her broken friend into her arms as Tess screamed.

CHAPTER ELEVEN

"Tess, My God, Tess, what is it?! Are you okay?" Jack was cradling Tess in his arms when she came to. She shook herself like a confused Newfoundland.

"What the hell Jack? Let go of me!" Tess shoved him away as she realized that she was in bed with only her underwear and bra on. Thor jumped up and began to vigorously lick her face. "Come on Thor, get down, jeez. Jack why am I half naked?" Tess enquired as she pushed Thor off the bed.

"Your top was covered in blood so I took it off. I promise there was no funny business, I didn't touch your lady-parts, well to be absolutely honest I did look at . . ." Jack's ramblings were cut short by a incensed Tess.

"You are detestable! First you drugged me; then you assaulted me when I was unconscious! What kind of a person . . ." Jack quickly interrupted her.

"Wait a second, I gave you half a pain pill, I can't help it if you passed out on that. Then I removed your bloody clothes, what a crime, then I put you in bed and watched out for you while you had the worst nightmare I have ever seen! I never touched you! But I will tell you this, someone did. No woman screams like that unless something beyond horrible happened to them. Now will you settle down and explain to me what I am really being blamed for?" Jack sat down next to the bed and tentatively placed his hand over Tess' shivering fingers.

And she did, long into the wee hours. Tess told Jack the story of that horrible night long ago and the effect it had on her life. The act of finally unburdening herself to another person had a deeply calming affect. As she uttered the last sentence and shed the last tear, she leaned her head against the pillows and closed her eyes in relief. Jack kicked off his shoes, climbed into bed and pulled her against him.

"So that explains the scars, both mental and physical. Tess I have to tell you that right now I hate my gender. It makes me sick when I think about what has happened to you and billions of women at the hands of men since the beginning of time. I promise you that there are men all over the world who would never consider hurting a woman. In fact, the majority of men love and respect women, you just don't hear about us regular guys as much as you do the monsters." Jack looked into Tess' eyes.

"Jack, please don't think that I am a man-hater. I have faith; I believe in the inherent goodness of mankind, no matter what I have witnessed. Most of all I trust you; you have been absolutely honest with me from the start, you saved my life and you are a decent and kind man." As Tess uttered these words she knew them to be true, she had stopped trying to manipulate Jack for her own purposes.

She had let down her guard with a man for the first time in her life. The feeling was exhilarating and strangely erotic. She grabbed Jack, rolled him on his back and began to remove his shirt.

"Whoa! Whoa! Hold on there little missy! I'm confused, one minute you are accusing me of assaulting you and the next you are assaulting me. What gives?" Jack pulled Tess' hands from his shirt.

"I want you, pure and simple. I don't want to think about it, I don't want to talk about it." Tess smiled as Jack hurriedly tore off his shirt.

"Okay, just so you know, this does not change anything. When my parents get here tomorrow we are getting on a conference call with President Thomson and you will agree to deliver the Blood." Jack ripped off Tess' bra and threw it over his head as he pinned her with a bruising kiss.

"Stop talking Jack!" Tess screamed as she wrapped her legs around him and dug her nails into his muscled back. Thor, thoroughly confused by the humans, jumped into a soft chair in the corner and fell asleep.

*   *   *

Thor's raucous snoring woke Tess up. She silently slipped out of bed, dressed, put the kettle on in the kitchen, raised the panels and let Thor out; all the while checking for bears. She observed that the dressing on her leg was soaked in blood as she smiled at the memories of last night.

In her wildest dreams she could never have imagined what real "love-making," was. To her sex was sex. What she and Jack had shared last night was beyond her understanding. She realized that Jack was deeply in love with her and she was very attracted to him. Unfortunately, none of that could be taken into consideration. She was leaving the country today and would never see Jack again.

Thor came bounding back in as Jack joined her in the kitchen. He had a rumpled little boy look about him that tore a hole in her heart. She steeled herself; she was good at that.

"I will cook this time, how about blueberry pancakes?" Tess moved around the kitchen organizing all of the ingredients as Jack peered at her through sleepy eyes.

"How can you be so perky? I am exhausted! I broke my personal best last night! Five times . . ." Jack raised his hand and wiggled his fingers " . . . five times in one session, I should be given a medal by some sort of Olympic committee."

Tess laughed as she mixed the batter and poured small rounds into the pan. "Jack it's two in the afternoon. I assume your parents will be here soon, we need to get ready." Tess flipped the pancakes, made the tea and handed the results to Jack. "I'm hitting the shower." She took a quick shower, changed the dressing on her wound and shoved her essentials into her purse as Jack joined her in the bathroom.

"Tess, I am going to trust you not to run while I am in here. Will you promise me?" Jack placed his hands on her shoulders and looked into her eyes.

"Jack I swear that I will wait for your parents and speak with President Thomson when the time comes." Tess left the room, closing the door behind her. She grabbed the bulging purse and ran downstairs. Desperately seeking a place to hide it, she finally decided to put it behind the giant stuffed Grizzly by the side door, just as a man and a woman entered through the front door.

Thor immediately ran to her side and began to bark out a warning. Tess had just enough time to register the fact that Jack's mom was tall, dark, gorgeous and obviously of Native American descent when Jack came down the stairs and enveloped her in a hug. Jack's dad was the same height as his son, thin as a rail, with a mop of brown curly hair atop his head. Jack hugged his father and turned to Tess.

"Tess this is my mom Nancy and my dad Dave. Mom, dad, this is Tess." Jack watched as they all shook hands, warily eyeing each other.

"Tess it is so nice to finally meet you. My son has been singing your praises for months. I am sorry that we have to meet under such trying circumstances." Nancy draped her arm around Tess' shoulder and steered her toward the couch. "Now why don't you just sit down and we can all have a reasonable talk." The men joined the women on the couches as Thor dropped down on top of Tess' feet.

"First off, I want to share with you what the U.S. government knows about your organization." Nancy looked around to see if anyone had something to say. Satisfied that she had the floor her continued. "Tess we know that you are the Keeper of the Flame. We know the Sisterhood has possession of the Flame and we know that the secret hiding place has been handed down generation to generation. We simply want you to retrieve it and give it to us so that we may present it to the Indian government. In exchange for your cooperation we will turn a blind eye to the involvement of your family and the Sisterhood in obtaining it. We will also agree to keep all information regarding the Sisterhood confidential."

Nancy continued, "We know the roots of your organization began with the fight for suffrage in the U.S. We have discovered that Sara immigrated to this country in August of 1913 and joined her friends Alice Paul and Lucy Burns. We have traced Sara's friendship with Paul and Burns back to England and the women's suffrage movement there. We assume that Sara brought the Flame with her and hid it somewhere in the Congressional Union for Woman Suffrage, or CU, headquarters." Nancy held up her hand as Tess shook her head.

"There is no use denying a direct connection between the British and American Suffragists, we have the government reports, signed by President Wilson, discussing the October 1913 U.S. speaking tour of Emmeline Pankhurst, the tour was sponsored by Harriot Stanton Blatch and the CU; we have photos of Sara at Pankhurst's Madison Square Garden speech on October 21. We also have photos of Sara working on The Suffragist, which was the weekly journal of the CU. To add to that, we have several photos of Sara with Dr. Anna Howard Shaw and her delegation of ninety-four women when they met with President Wilson on December 8, 1913." Nancy looked to Tess for her reaction.

At that moment Tess decided that she needed to get out of the house soon. She would stay to find out any information the government had on the Sisterhood and then make her escape. She assumed that the extraction team would create a diversion when it was time to leave. She would stay put, appear to cooperate and then bolt when the signal came.

Dave began to speak as she readied her plans. "Tess we don't want you to feel as if we are ganging up on you. I realize that you are a smart and capable woman. We all know that you let yourself be kidnapped in order to ascertain the depth of knowledge the gang had regarding the Sisterhood and the Flame. Luckily for the Sisterhood, Nathan and the Russian government don't appear to know about your organization, however, various nations seemed to have zeroed in on you. The intel that we are picking up has increased dramatically over the past few weeks and now it has reached a critical juncture. For your own sake, you must give us the Flame."

Tess had to hand it to the Avery's, they were very proficient at playing good cop, bad cop. "Dave you are absolutely right about everything . . ." Tess smiled inwardly as the other three visibly relaxed. Jack go up and banged around in the kitchen for a few minutes, then he returned with a platter of cold cuts, bread, grapes and several glasses filled with water. "I did let myself be taken, I am very interested in what the U.S. government knows about our organization, however, I have decided, in light of the threat against me, to cooperate with you and hand over the Flame. It has brought a lot of heat, pardon the pun, to the Sisterhood and I want it gone."

Tess realized that the Sisterhood would have to cut their loses on the Flame. She had every intention of honoring her word, just not on the U.S. government's terms. She had to escape, get to New Zealand and retrieve the Flame all the while keeping the location of the headquarters a secret.

It was best to turn the Flame over to the rightful owners; the people of India should have their treasured ruby. As of that moment Tess needed to find out two things, if Jack and his parents knew the whereabouts of their headquarters and if they believed the Flame was the only jewel in the satchel.

Nancy pulled a sheaf of papers from her briefcase. "Tess I want you to see the information that we have on the Sisterhood so you realize the extent of our knowledge. We have evidence that Sara joined with Paul and Burns to work on the suffrage amendment. We know that the younger generation was much more radical and they became even more so after the death of Inez Milholland in Los Angeles during her campaign tour for suffrage. They formed the National Woman's Party, or NWP, and began to picket the White House."

Tess took the papers from Nancy, shuffled them around and began to speak. "I realize that you have all of this information on Sara. Don't you understand? Can't you see what these women went through? Sara, and other members of the NWP, were attacked by men on the sidewalk in front of the White House; arrested on trumped up charges of 'obstructing traffic' and then thrown into the Occoquan Workhouse. In Occoquan they were beaten and Lucy Burns was handcuffed with her arms above her head all night!" Tears began to form in Tess' eyes.

Jack stood up, gathered Tess in his arms and sat with her on the couch opposite his parents. "Look Tess, we do understand. I told you that we have all seen Iron Jawed Angels. We saw the beatings. We watched the hunger strikers force-fed with tubes shoved down their mouths and noses; I was gagging the entire scene. Alice Paul, Lucy Burns, Dora Lewis, Julia Emory, Rose Winslow and Sara, they were all heroines. We have done an enormous amount of research regarding the suffrage movement. We even read Doris Stevens' Jailed for Freedom."

Tess leaned back into Jack. She would miss this close sense of companionship; a feeling she had never enjoyed before. "I know, I know, it just . . . well it still hurts. I can't explain it. I feel sad and angry and frustrated and lost all at the same time. Whenever I think about those poor women and what they went through. The courage that it took to endure the beatings and torture." She visibly shook herself and moved a bit away from Jack; better to get some distance.

"So how did everyone find me? I thought Sara did a pretty good job of covering her tracks." Tess turned toward Nancy.

Nancy obliged. "It all began with Rose Winslow. She and Sara had gone out to Wyoming in 1916, with the support of the newly formed National Woman's Party, to campaign for the federal amendment before they were arrested for picketing. Because of the campaigning and torture they became fast friends. In her diary Winslow described a meeting that she and Sara had attended, in Wyoming, in which they met a cousin of Jeannette Rankin's named Clement. Winslow went on to describe what an 'amiable' man he was and the fact that Sara seemed to be 'quite taken' with him. Once we had a name, we went back into the marriage records and discovered that Clement Rankin had married a Sara Smith in the autumn of 1920." Nancy looked to Tess for confirmation.

"Yes, that is all correct. Sara changed her last name when she arrived in the U.S. and fell in love with Clement when she was campaigning in Wyoming. According to my nana, Sara liked the idea of living in the state that was the first to grant women the vote." Tess realized that she needed to get Thor to her team.

He would not be able to accompany her to New Zealand because of the strict anti-rabies quarantine laws. She got up off the coach and pushed Thor out the front door. He immediately began to bark, in order to distract Jack and his parents she went into professor mode.

"Right, where were we? The first legislature to introduce a women's suffrage bill was Washington Territory in 1848, the same year as the Seneca Falls Convention, that bill was defeated, however, on December 10, 1869, Wyoming became the first territory to grant women the right to vote. On September 30, 1889, Wyoming approved the first state constitution that included suffrage for women. Sara and Clement were extremely proud of that historic achievement. People tend to think that the eastern seaboard was the front-runner as far as women's rights went, but by 1914 all of the states west of the Rockies had women's suffrage." As Tess took a breath, Nancy's cell made a beeping sound.

Nancy pushed a button and spoke into her phone. "Senator Avery, yes we are ready, thank you." She placed the phone on the coffee table, stood up and walked to the side of the fireplace. She pressed a discreet button on one of the stones and a huge projection screen lowered from the ceiling.

An image flickered then came into focus as Tess realized she was looking at the president of the United States of America. Tess jumped up from the couch and faced the screen. President Thomson had long chestnut colored hair that cascaded down her back, flawless skin, full red lips and emerald green eyes.

Those eyes were flashing in anger as her voice ripped through the speakers in the room. "So this is the woman who drug our country into this unholy mess. Before we begin the interrogation Dr. Rankin, I want you to know that all deals are off the table! You killed a man in front of several witnesses and you are going to prison for murder!"

CHAPTER TWELVE

Deb looked at the two women in front of her wondering if you had to be drop-dead gorgeous to belong to the Sisterhood. Liz paced back and forth like a caged panther, her black hair swinging across her back. Leigh-Anne was the exact opposite. She sat like a goddess on her throne.

Her piercing ice-blue eyes, golden skin, glorious blonde mane and youthful appearance belied the fact that she was the CEO of the Sisterhood. Deb was trying to take in all of the information that the two women had provided, however, after an eighteen-hour flight, she was wilting.

"Deb, I am so sorry that we have dumped all of this on you when you are jet lagged . . ." Leigh-Anne locked her eyes on Deb's. "But we are trying to impress upon you the need for secrecy. We will let you contact your husband and father after we have a short talk. Basically, we are asking you to stay with us for several weeks, until the beginning of summer in mid December, when the lake level drops so that Tess can dive to an underwater cave and collect the Flame. Tess trusts you completely and you have a certain skill set that we need for the mission."

Deb barked out a laugh as she resettled her lanky frame on the plush sofa. She assumed that the term "skill set" was a euphemism for her ability to use a gun. From the moment she was met at LAX by a terrifyingly efficient giant of a man named Weston, Deb knew she was about to embark upon some sort of dangerous assignment.

She had been prepared to purchase a ticket under Liz's name, however, Weston approached her and explained the change in plans. Weston was an amazing specimen of manhood. Deb assumed from his massive size and dark coloring that he was of Maori descent.

She had been unceremoniously escorted to a private jet, settled in and flown more than halfway around the world. She had been silently served food, drinks and reading materials (all of the books were about the history of New Zealand) at various intervals. Upon arrival in Queenstown, she had checked into The Dairy hotel under the watchful eyes of the proprietors/chefs, Matt and Paul, and then had been promptly whisked away by Liz after a brief introduction.

She looked out of the floor to ceiling windows toward Lake Wakatipu at the foot of The Remarkables mountain range. Deb had learned a good deal about New Zealand during her long flight. She had never realized that the country was actually two islands, the North Island and the South Island that were separated by Cook Strait, and that the population was around five million. Farming was a major occupation, however, tourism was flourishing, especially after Peter Jackson had used the North and South islands as a stand-in for Middle Earth with his filming of the Lord of the Rings Trilogy and The Hobbit.

Most of the population was of European descent, however, the indigenous people, the Maori, were a resurgent and vibrant community. There were also a number of Asian and Pacific Islanders. The most impressive statistic the Deb had come across was the fact that New Zealand had a ninety-nine percent adult literacy rate. The majority of the population lived on the North Island, centered around the major cities of Auckland, Christchurch and Wellington.

Queenstown was considered the "Jewel" of the South Island. It was a breathtakingly beautiful city. With The Remarkables looming over the town, it reminded Deb of Switzerland. Deb had seen the director Jane Campion's mystery series, Top of the Lake, which made Queenstown feel a bit more familiar.

Winter was summer and summer was winter in the Southern Hemisphere so the current temps were ranging between sixty to seventy degrees Fahrenheit with about seventy percent humidity. The odd weather was adding to her feeling of disorientation, Deb's wondering thoughts were cut short by Leigh-Anne.

"As I was saying, Lake Wakatipu is a glacial lake that is fifty miles long and over a thousand feet deep. Tess placed the Flame in an underwater cave by Hidden Island, which is in the middle of the lake. The diving conditions are extreme and unpredictable. In December of 2010 two men were found dead near Hidden Island. That lake is nothing to muck about with." As Leigh-Anne continued on about Pig Island, Pigeon Island and Tree Island, Deb was attempting to pull a memory regarding Lake Wakatipu. Try as she might, she could not place the context, other than the Campion series. She had a nagging suspicion that the lost memory was regarding something scary and dangerous.

"Deb, have I lost you?" Leigh-Anne waved her hand in front of Deb's face. "Okay, Liz will explain the diving part and then you can make your calls and get some sleep."

"Alright Deb, I am going to walk you through what we will be up to for the next few weeks. You are a beginner diver; an average dive for you would be ten to fifteen meters. Experienced recreational divers would generally max out at thirty meters, which is about ninety feet; any deeper than that and you run the risk of needing decompression stops or time in a decompression chamber. When Tess arrives she will train you to do a deep dive. Here are some cherries, strawberries and apricots, they are amazing this time of year." Liz handed Deb a plate of fruit.

"Where was I? So the dive we are talking about will be over thirty meters, around one hundred feet. You and Tess will descend slowly through those intervals, what do you call them?" Liz looked to Deb.

"Atmospheres." Deb answered.

"Right, atmospheres, so you can equalize the pressure in your ears. It will take roughly five minutes to get down. Seven minutes in the cave, grab the Flame, slowly ascend including the safety stop at five meters from the surface for a few minutes and you should have plenty of air in your tanks. Weston and I will be topside handling the boat. We expect Tess to arrive in a couple of days; she will need forty-eight hours, just to be on the safe side, before she begins to train you. There are only three people who know where the Flame is hidden. Leigh-Anne and I are too claustrophobic to dive and we are counting on you to accompany Tess. Will you help us?" Liz handed Deb a glass of water and joined her on the couch.

As Deb devoured her plate of fruit she considered her position. She knew that she would agree to stay and help. When Leigh-Anne had explained the history of the Sisterhood, the Flame and Tess' involvement, Deb had looked around for a hidden camera. She quickly realized the veracity of Leigh-Anne's claims when Liz gave her a dossier to read.

It was wildly improbable, funny, sad, frightening and heroic. The tale was also true. Deb was hooked; perhaps for the rest of her life. She really didn't know what she was signing on for.

"I'm in. I will help Tess dive for the Flame, she and I will bring it back to the U.S. and convince my dad to contact his friends in D.C., then we will personally turn it over to President Thomson herself. Now if I understand the dossier correctly, this entire process began in England in 1792 when Mary Wollstonecraft wrote Vindication of the Rights of Woman. Besides being the mother of Mary Shelley, who wrote Frankenstein, Wollstonecraft was an ardent feminist. That's why this place is called Wollstonecraft House. She inspired Elizabeth Cady Stanton, Susan B. Anthony and Lucretia Mott. That led to Sara Jones joining Alice Paul and Lucy Burns. Those three hid the Flame somewhere in Cameron House the National Woman's Party headquarters." Deb looked on as Leigh-Anne and Liz bobbed their heads in unison.

"Okay, I just have two questions: what is the significance of the yellow rose and why the hell are you headquartered in New Zealand?" Deb smiled as Liz laughed.

"Easy, peasy, our secret, for lack of a better word, headquarters are here in New Zealand because in 1893 this country became the first in the world to grant universal suffrage. The first country to give women the right to vote deserved our support and investment. We have offices in San Francisco and New York City because those two in particular are leaders in human and civil rights. The yellow rose was worn by Suffragists during the fight for the ratification of the Nineteenth, or Susan B. Anthony, Amendment, the yellow rose has become a precious symbol of the fight for equality for women." Liz looked at Deb and continued to speak.

"Alex and Theo will help you with your phone calls. You might recognize them as the students that went missing. After Tess and her yummy sidekick Jack left the scene, our retrieval team found the guys and gave them a brief explanation of what had actually transpired. They immediately offered to help us with our tech department. I think they envisioned dozens of women working in a secret lair. We decided to bring them aboard and they have been invaluable to us. They will route your calls through so many countries that no one will be able to trace them." Just as Liz finished, two ruggedly handsome young men entered.

Deb stood up, walked over to them and smacked their heads together. "My dad has been working his tail off looking for you two bozos. I suggest you use your super secret phone routing system to call your parents, the university and anyone else foolish enough to care about you."

"Yeesh, lady, you sound just like our mom, and we don't even know you." Theo rubbed his head as Alex laughed.

"Didn't your parents teach you to use your words not your fists! Obviously you have been out of touch, we contacted everyone who cares about us and told them we moved to San Francisco to work for a tech startup. Now if you are done assaulting us we will take you to our office." Alex performed a deeply dramatic bow as Deb laughingly followed the brothers out of the room.

Leigh-Anne sat on the couch and turned to Liz. "So what do you think? Can we trust Deb?"

"We can trust anyone that Tess puts her absolute faith in. I believe that Deb will help us now and possibly in the future. She is a valuable asset. I am concerned about the fact that we have several governments, and who knows how many rouge agents, trying to find the Flame. For the first time since the Sisterhood began, the true nature of our mission is in jeopardy. We have got to get rid of the Flame before someone finds out that we are more than a charitable organization dedicated to empowering women and girls around the globe." Liz stood up and gazed out of the windows that offered a magnificent view of the lake and mountains.

Leigh-Anne joined Liz at the windows. "You are so right. We have to get rid of that cursed ruby. Our organization has survived and thrived for over a hundred years because we kept a low profile, now that is in danger. Liz, I have a very bad feeling about this situation. We need to get Tess back and work on Deb's deep dives. The sooner we get the Flame to D.C. the better it will be for all of us."

Liz rested her hand on Leigh-Anne's shoulder. "Don't worry, it will all go according to plan. The only problem I foresee is with Jack. From everything we have overheard, he is crazy about Tess and he seems to be fairly determined and resourceful. When we retrieve her, he won't just let her go, and he has the backing of the U.S. government. Of course he really doesn't know Tess, when she is cornered she will turn and fight."

CHAPTER THIRTEEN

"Whoa, whoa, whoa!" Tess backed away from the huge screen and moved closer to the Grizzly bear. Things were turning sour faster than she had anticipated; time to go. "I didn't kill anybody! You can ask Jack, he was right there. What do you mean witnesses?" Tess looked up at the screen as Jack rose to her defense.

"President Thomson, I don't know who you spoke with but Tess didn't kill Nathan. The shot came from outside the window. We saw it all." Jack moved closer to Tess as President Thomson spoke.

"I received my intel from a field agent. That is what she told me. Jack, if you will attest to Tess' innocence I believe you. I can promise you that we did not kill Nathan. It must have been someone from the Sisterhood. With that being the case, we will need to investigate your organization." President Thomson rested her searing gaze on Tess.

"Wait, there is no need to blackmail us Madame President. We will give you the Flame as soon as I . . ." Tess was interrupted by President Thomson.

"Young woman, the President of the United States does not blackmail citizens!"

"Pardon me Madame President, I didn't mean to imply that you were threatening me or the Sisterhood. Especially when we have been such loyal financial supporters of your various campaigns during your distinguished career." Tess suppressed a smirk as the screen went blank and President Thomson could be heard whispering in the background. After a few moments she returned looking ashen.

"I have just been informed that your organization has supported me to the tune of one million dollars over the years. While I am deeply grateful for your generous backing, I will not submit to your blackmail." President Thomson let the threat hang in the air as Nancy jumped in.

"Please, let's all just calm down." Nancy rested her hand on Tess' shoulder and gently squeezed it. This simple gesture immediately brought tears to Tess' eyes. Her mother had done the same thing when she was a hot-headed child. Tess turned away from the group and steeled herself for the final negotiation as Nancy continued.

"Madame President, no one is trying to blackmail you. The Sisterhood has generously given its support to a number of women's political campaigns, including my own, over the years. We are all in agreement here. Let's just put the removal of Nathan down as a mystery and go from there." Tess turned back to the screen and imperceptibly moved closer to the side door by the Grizzly bear.

"As long as I don't need to explain anything about Nathan's disappearance to the Russians, I agree. From the report I have on him he sounds like a nasty piece of work. Now Tess, let's discuss the retrieval of the Flame. We will not negotiate with you; this transaction will go according to our terms. You will tell us where the Flame is hidden and we will send a team to get it. You will not be allowed within miles of the ruby and your organization will be monitored to make sure they comply." President Thomson leaned across her massive desk in the Oval Office and locked eyes with Tess. "Is that understood?"

"Yes, Madame President." Tess had decided to go along with whatever the president suggested and then escape after she rang off. "I promise you that the Sisterhood will turn over the Flame. We just want to get the ruby back to the rightful owner and be left in peace to pursue our mission." She was not exactly lying, the Sisterhood would give the jewel to the Indian government; they simply wouldn't go along with President Thomson's scenario.

"Good. Wait a moment. Jack, what did you mean by we? Who else was in the room when Nathan was killed?" President Thomson peered at Jack.

"Alex and Theo, the two computer students who worked with Nathan and I. I thought you had them?" Jack looked at the screen.

"No we don't have them. We thought you just used them for support and paid them off. I don't know where they are, but they are not with us. Our agents searched the cabin and the only thing they found was Nathan's body. The agents left in a hurry as the local sheriff arrived on the scene. We need to find those young men and debrief them. You wouldn't know anything about their whereabouts would you Dr. Rankin?" Tess was honestly mystified. She hadn't a clue as to where Alex and Theo had gone.

"Madam President, I assure you that I don't know anything about my students. I am as worried as you are. They are nice guys and I wouldn't want anything to happen to them." Tess could not account for their disappearance. Under normal circumstances, the guys should have headed toward town. If that had been the case then Sheriff Mike would have picked them up.

"I will have my agents begin a search. Don't worry, we will find them and bring them in for questioning regarding the events that took place in the cabin. Now to insure that your organization does not get creative, Jack will bring you to the White House and you will be my guest while the negotiations are taking place. I look forward to continuing our discussion later on this evening." President Thomson pushed a button and the screen went blank.

Wow. President Thomson was a "take no prisoners" kind of woman; Tess actually admired her for that. She hoped that her next move would not make an enemy of such a formidable woman. Tess walked toward the side door and switched on the inside lights as Nancy and Dave began to turn on lights around the room. Tess was moments away from escaping; she was just waiting for a signal from the Sisterhood.

Nancy must have sensed a change in Tess. "Now Tess why don't you sit down and relax for a few moments before you and Jack leave. Considering the fact that my son seems to be in love with you I think you owe him the courtesy of telling him who you really are." Tess jumped at the realization that Nancy had a good deal more information regarding Tess' field ops than anyone had let on.

"I don't know what you mean by that Nancy. I am simply a professor and a member of the Sisterhood." Tess knew where this was heading and she assumed that she would be retrieved in a matter of seconds considering the path that they were on.

"Wait, mom, what are you talking about? I don't understand." Jack turned to look at Tess as Nancy continued.

"Honey, Tess is what is referred to as a Flame Thrower. She is an assassin for the Sisterhood. She might not have killed Nathan, however, she has killed other men. Isn't that right Tess?" Nancy looked at Tess as Jack spoke.

"Tess, tell my mom that's not true. Tell her you are not a, what did she call you, a Flame Thrower." Jack begged Tess as she looked sadly into his eyes. He read her expression wordlessly. Tess almost stepped toward him in an attempt to explain, then she stopped herself, it was better this way. Jack needed to see who she really was.

The life that Tess led had no place for a man like Jack. Tess had given herself body and soul to a cause that on occasion turned violent. Tess had killed men, many men, when she had been forced to protect herself and the lives of innocent women and children. She also knew that there was no way Nancy could have known this unless she sat on the board of the Sisterhood.

Tess understood Nancy's concern. She knew that the last thing Nancy wanted was for her son to love a Flame Thrower. Tess realized that Nancy would tell Dave and Jack that she had obtained the information from the president and they would never know she was a member of the Sisterhood. Tess would keep her secret. It was her job to keep secrets. If Nancy was trying to protect the Sisterhood by devastating her own son, so be it.

As the horrible truth sunk in, Jack's expression changed from desperation to anguish. He uttered one word, "no" before the lights went out.

Tess grabbed her bag from behind the Grizzly bear and raced out the door as Thor began to howl. She could hear Jack, Dave and Nancy all shouting within the house and the sounds of stomping boots on the ground. She ran for the river hoping that the Sisterhood would track her signal and meet her by the banks. As she rounded a corner by a rock outcropping a vice-like grip grabbed her from behind. She turned to look into a pair of unfamiliar eyes.

"Dr. Rankin, you will come with us please. We are not going to hurt you. You have something that belongs to our country and we want it back. I can assure you that no harm will befall you."

Two men and two women, who were obviously of Indian descent, surrounded Tess. She had just enough time to think, "now what," when the men picked her up, pulled a bag over her head, and ran off. She was unceremoniously tossed into the back seat of a vehicle, which sped off into the night.

CHAPTER FOURTEEN

"Will everyone just stop talking and sit down!" Sheriff Mike's voice echoed through the suddenly quiet office. "Now Dr. Avery is trying to explain to us what is going on, let him finish and then we can all ask questions." Sheriff Mike dropped into a chair as Miz Robinson, Mason, Edward, Robyn and Gregg Redhawk followed suit.

Jack looked around at the rustic setting. The weak sun shone through the dust- covered windows of the station. A person entered the work area by pushing through a set of short swinging doors that reminded Jack of an old western saloon. He imagined that the only time the two cells were occupied would be on weekend nights. Every inch of the station reminded him of the old Andy Griffith show.

"Please call me Jack, as I was saying, this discussion can't go beyond these walls. I know the entire story that I have told you seems implausible at best and impossible at worst, but I assure you that every word is true. Right now Tess and Deb are in extreme danger and I thought all of you might be able to help. So Mr. Redhawk, I got your cell number from

Mike. That is Greg with two G's?" Jack joined the rest of the group in their circle of chairs, as Thor settled at his feet. When Tess had disappeared from the house Thor had fiercely attached himself to Jack. They had been inseparable ever since.

"Nope, three G's. So you are saying that Tess and Deb are looking for the Flame right now and you don't have any idea where they are?" Gregg stretched his boot-clad feet and denim covered legs in front of him. "Considering that you have the resources of the entire U.S. government behind you, that is a pretty piss poor result. Listen Jack . . ." Gregg seemed to hiss when he pronounced Jack's name, "our toddlers on the reservation could do a better tracking job than that. Let me show you something." Gregg motioned for the group to follow him as he moved to Miz Robinson's computer.

"Look here." Gregg was pointing to a couple of people on the screen. Mike's CIA buddy had sent him endless hours of film footage taken from the cameras at the airport in L.A. the day Deb disappeared.

"Let me blow this up. If you look carefully, even though the woman has on sunglasses, a ball cap and her jacket collar is turned up, you can tell by the way she walks that we are looking at Deb. Notice that she and the big guy with her are heading toward the private plane section of the airport.

Obviously they boarded a plane to somewhere. I don't know how they got around the passport check but they managed it. If you ask me, that big dude is the key to where in the hell she is; I gotta say that he looks familiar. I just can't place him right now." Gregg straightened up from his position at the desk and walked toward the swinging doors.

"Now I have a ranch to run, Jack if I think of anything I'll call you." With a tip of his cowboy hat Gregg pushed through the doors and walked out of the building. Jack watched as Gregg got into a shiny new pickup. Gregg was a formidable character. He was well over six feet with a ramrod straight bearing. Between the Native American coloring and his general swagger, Jack found him intimidating. Looking back on all of the times Jack had broken into Tess' house, he was relieved that he had never accidentally run into Gregg. Armed with a knife, it looked as if Gregg would have happily sliced open Jack stem to stern.

"Okay, that is where we will begin. Mason and Edward, look at every bit of footage again. Robyn get on over to the university and see if you can follow up on those two missing boys, I still think they are somehow linked to all of this." Mike motioned for Jack to follow him to his office as Miz Robinson settled back at her computer.

"We need to talk." Mike waited for Jack to sit in one of the two chairs facing the sheriff's desk while Thor, once again, remained at Jack's side, then he closed the door. Mike dropped down in his chair behind his desk and carefully studied Jack.

"Alright son, I can tell by the desperation in your voice and your hang-dog look that you are in love with Tess so I will cut you some slack and half believe your cockamamie story." Mike liked to get a person riled up when he was interrogating them, anger made people sloppy.

"I am in love with Tess, however, every word I spoke is true. I put my entire professional future on the line because I shared this with all of you. If President Thomson finds out I divulged secret government information I can kiss my career good-bye. She will make my life a living hell. I need the people closest to Tess to help me figure out where she is, that's why I took a chance and came here. Now are you going to work with me or not?" Jack leaned forward to emphasize his point.

Mike looked him up and down; Jack seemed legit. He was the son of a senator and had direct contact with President Thomson. That had been easy enough to check when Jack first arrived at the station. There was also an indefinable air of trustworthiness about Jack.

Mike decided that his desperation to find Deb and Tess trumped his natural skepticism. Besides he could always lock him up and call the Feds if he became a problem.

"Okay, Jack. I have decided to trust you, for now. I want you to stay at the Rankin Ranch with Gregg and see what you two come up with, rip her place apart if you have to, just find us anything. We will follow every lead we can from here. If Edward and Mason discover anything on the airport footage we will let you know. I realize that when you ran from your parents' home, after Tess disappeared, it put you in a tough spot. We will keep your secret and not let anyone know you are here." Mike watched as Jack seemed to struggle with something and then he began to speak.

"I appreciate that sheriff. I do have another lead I would like you to follow up, if you would. According to my research, after the 19th Amendment was passed Alice Paul dedicated her life to the Equal Rights Amendment. You know about the ERA right?" Jack looked at Mike.

"Yes, Jack. This is not no-where land; I even went to college. The ERA states, 'Equality of rights under the law shall not be denied or abridged by the United States or by any state on account of sex.' So what does that have to do with locating Deb and Tess?" Mike gave Jack a bemused look.

"Sorry, I didn't mean to question your intellectual capabilities. What I am trying to explain is that Alice Paul moved out of the U.S. for a time and in 1938 she established the World Woman's Party or WWP. The WWP headquarters were in Geneva, Switzerland. Tess mentioned something about having a Swiss bank account. I can get a friend to look into that angle. I need you to follow up on another lead. According to my research both Alice Paul and Christabel Pankhurst lived in California for a time. In fact, Pankhurst died in Santa Monica in 1958. The Sisterhood has offices in San Francisco and New York City. Could you get someone to poke around the SF office? Two of the most powerful women in the suffrage movement living in California and the Sisterhood office in SF seems like more than a coincidence to me." Jack got up and leaned over to shake Mike's hand.

"Okay Jack I will check into the SF office. You go on ahead and get back to the ranch and help Gregg. Oh wait a sec, what was the name of the organization that you said has all the info on Alice Paul?" Mike picked up a pen and grabbed a nearby yellow legal pad.

"Right, it is called the Alice Paul Institute. You can find them online. They are located in Mount Laurel, New Jersey at Paulsdale, which is the home where Alice Paul was born. The API is loaded with great info on all of the Suffragists. I have visited their website many times." With that shared, Jack and Thor got up and headed out the door.

As he drove back toward the Rankin Ranch, or the Double R, as it was called by the locals; he absentmindedly scratched Thor's head and considered his options. He could contact his parents and work with the U.S. government or he could continue on with Tess' people. Even with all of the formidable search capabilities of the government, Jack's instincts told him, that the Sisterhood had been so successful for such a long time because it kept itself low tech.

He suspected that they had a state-of-the-art IT department, however, when it came to individuals he had a sense that all of the various, for lack of a better word, agents communicated with the headquarters on disposable cell phones or by some other very discreet means. He pulled up to the front door of Tess' home and knocked. Gregg answered looking none too pleased to see him.

"What do you want Jack?" Gregg stood with his arms crossed.

"Look Gregg, we got off to a rocky start. Sheriff Mike wants me to stay here and help you search for clues. I promise that I only have Tess' safety as my motive. Please let me try." Jack put out his hand. Gregg shrugged and grasped his hand in a bone-crushing shake.

"Alright, I will let you stay here, as long as you are useful. Come on in." Gregg stepped aside and let Jack and Thor into the house. "I found a safe and I have been inputting numbers but so far no luck. Do you know any numbers that might work?" Gregg showed Jack into the library where a panel behind a bookcase stood open as Thor happily bounded around the house looking for his favorite chicken squeaky toy.

Once again Jack had a chance to admire the stunning old farmhouse. With its Victorian bay windows and towers, wraparound porch, delicate woodwork trimmings and forest green color with burgundy trim it belonged on the cover of Architectural Digest. The downstairs consisted of a massive kitchen, which stretched across the back of the house, a formal dining room outfitted with gleaming walnut furniture, a parlor filled with comfy stuffed leather chairs and couches in various shades of burgundy and cream and a library.

Jack looked around the library and appreciated the floor to ceiling cherry wood bookcases. In the back of the library facing out from the bookcases stood a massive mahogany desk covered with papers. This was the library of a professor. Jack walked over to the open panel and stood next to Gregg. "So you tried all of the usual numbers, birthdays, anniversaries, etc?"

"Yep." Was all he got out of Gregg.

"Okay, how about suffrage numbers. What would you say would be the most important dates in the suffrage movement?" Jack turned to Gregg.

"Well I already keyed in the dates for Seneca Falls and 1924 when Nellie Tayloe Ross was elected governor of Wyoming. Since she was the first woman governor in the U.S. and from Wyoming I thought that might work. I also tried the date the guy from Tennessee changed his vote and supported ratification of the 19th Amendment. What was that guy's name?" Gregg looked as if it was right on the tip of his tongue. Jack was not surprised at Gregg's knowledge. Anyone who worked for Tess' family would know the history of the suffrage movement.

"Burn, Harry Burn. His mother was Febb Ensminger Burn, a college graduate, which for that time was a huge deal. Mrs. Burn, of Mouse Creek, Tennessee, wrote the famous letter to her son urging him to vote for ratification. He stated, 'I know that a mother's advice is always safest for her boy to follow,' and then he voted 'yea' and that one vote granted universal suffrage to American women. I have got to agree with him on the mother's advice aspect. Many times I wish I had followed that path. So Representative Burn voted and Tennessee finally ratified the 19th Amendment on August 24, 1920. Was that the date you used?" Jack scratched his head absentmindedly as Gregg nodded.

145

"Alright, let's try August 26, 1920, the date that Secretary of State Bainbridge Colby signed the 19th Amendment into law. It is known as Equality Day, maybe that is it." Jack punched the numbers into the keypad, the safe beeped three times and the door swung open. Gregg reached his hands in and pulled out dozens of files and a shortwave radio.

"Wait what am I looking at? Is that a shortwave radio? I have only seen those in movies." Jack watched as Gregg set up the files and the radio on a clear table under the window.

"Wow, this is really old school. A shortwave radio, oh man Jack, I think I know why Tess has this." Gregg turned the nobs as the radio came to life. "Have you ever heard of Number Stations?" Jack shook his head as Gregg continued. "They are a relic of the Cold War; I heard a program about them on National Public Radio. According to the guy on NPR these stations were heavily used in Cuba right after Castro came to power." Gregg looked to see if Jack was following his explanation.

"So how this works is, the shortwave radio spectrum is used to transmit secret messages by hundreds of Number Stations. The spies would use a One-Time-Pad encryption system that was unbreakable. It was untraceable because two people would have pads that had the same numbers and once they were used they would destroy them. Think of it as a string of numbers that belong to a dictionary for a language that would be spoken just one time. So the Sisterhood could effectively communicate with their operatives using a device that has absolutely nothing to do with the 21st Century. These women found a way to completely circumvent the computer age. It is genius!" Gregg continued to examine the shortwave radio as Jack opened the first file and spoke.

"Nothing would surprise me, if they are all like Tess. It's kinda amazing to think of a vast network of female agents, dedicated to women's rights, scouring the globe looking to correct injustices against women and children. They must be like super heroes or should I say super heroines. My mom called Tess a Flame Thrower; she said it means that Tess is an assassin. Do you believe that?" Jack looked to Gregg.

"Look Jack, you said it yourself. If the Sisterhood's mission is to protect women and children that can't defend themselves who do you think they need protection from? Us. Men. Traditionally we are the aggressors. We beat, rape and kill women and children. I say if Tess and her Flame Throwers knock off a few bad guys, the world would be a better place." Gregg pulled a chair to the table and continued to work with the radio.

"Gregg, that is not right. If that is the case they are little more than vigilantes." Jack grabbed a chair and joined Gregg at the table.

"Nope that is where you are wrong Jack. If Tess and her Flame Throwers really do spend their time going into dangerous situations to save women and children then they are at risk and they must do whatever it takes to defend themselves and their charges. I don't have a problem with that. In fact, if she asked me I would go along and help her." Gregg pulled a Swiss Army knife from his jean's pocket and began to unscrew the back of the radio.

"Well no matter what she is and what she does I am all in. I can't be in a world without her." Jack rested his head in his hands.

"Yea, I kinda got that back at the station. Look man, you seem like a decent guy. You come from a good family, you have a substantial income and it seems as if you are willing to move heaven and earth to find Tess and help her, so I will help you. You have to know that her decision is final. When we find her and get her out of this mess then she can figure everything out about you. Right now let's see if there are any clues in these files." Gregg stopped fiddling with the radio and began to scour the files.

"Got it, I just need you to do one thing for me." Jack raised his head and looked at Gregg.

"You name it." Gregg answered.

"Help me figure out who killed Nathan. If the U S government didn't do it and Tess said the Sisterhood didn't kill him, then we have another very dangerous player in the mix."

CHAPTER FIFTEEN

Tess squirmed as she was hoisted from the car and carried into what looked to be an abandoned warehouse. The hood had been pulled off upon her arrival, however, her hands and feet were duck taped, blood was slowly seeping from her bandaged leg.

She assumed that her captors were not worried that she might be able to identify where she was. It seemed as if the warehouse was some sort of old granary, judging from the wheaty smell and the large silo at the far end.

Opaque light from the street lamps filtered in through grime-encrusted windows. The vast interior was empty except for several stacks of wooden pallets and various rusty unrecognizable machines. She was gently deposited on a decrepit looking couch as she continued to try and gain her bearings.

She knew they were still in Montana, considering the fact that they had only been in the car about an hour. She had frantically looked around outside before she was brought into the interior, however, none of the landmarks looked familiar. They were in a sparsely populated area that consisted of dimly lit shadowy buildings.

Oddly enough the landscape and the building reminded her of the show Warehouse 13. Tess almost smiled remembering the wonderful times she had with her colleagues Tristan and Patty watching their favorite show. Tristan taught computer science and Patty was an astronomy professor. Many a winter's night, Tristan, Patty and Tess had hunkered down in Tess' library, fortified with snacks, to watch Warehouse 13.

If Gregg's wife Serena was working late at the hospital, she was the go-to doctor in the emergency room, then he might join their party. Lately Tristan and been mentioning a new engineering professor quite a bit, judging by the way he described her, Tess expected that she would make an appearance soon. Patty was dating an astrophysicist. More and more Tess felt the isolation of being single.

As she squirmed up to a sitting position, Tess looked at her four captors with undisguised interest. By their accents and gorgeous coloring they seemed to be Indian. Tess had always loved the way people from India spoke English. They turned what was essentially an abrupt language into something more musical. Dressed head to foot in tight black clothing they were unbelievably attractive and lithe. She wondered if it was a requirement of the Indian special forces. There was no question in her mind that they were Indian military, the way they held themselves telegraphed special training.

"Dr. Rankin, we want you to know that we will not harm you. In fact, we will only hold you for a few moments. We just want your assurance that you will retrieve the Blood of India and deliver it to our government. Let me re-wrap your injured leg." One of the women assured her with a friendly smile as she deftly knelt down and replaced the soiled bandage with a fresh dressing. Then she removed the cap from a bottle of water and gently placed it into Tess' restricted hands.

"Thanks for the water and the expert nursing. I promise. By that I mean you have my word. I will recover the Flame or Blood, whatever, and return it to you. If you provide me with a way to contact you once I have it." Tess fully intended to keep her word. It was time. The Flame was a liability that the Sisterhood could no longer afford. It had brought too much scrutiny upon the organization.

"Could you please explain how you knew I had it?" Tess inquired.

"One of the librarians at the university in Mumbai contacted us when Dr. Avery began poking about in the archives that concerned the Blood. We placed him on a watch list hoping he might succeed where we had been stymied in our search, when he was attacked by several Russian thugs it confirmed our hopes. We followed him to Wyoming and observed while he and his cohorts attempted to abduct you. Their bungling was something out of a Bollywood film." She paused while the four of them heartily laughed at Jack.

"We don't know who you really are and we don't care. According to our research, you are a historian who travels extensively. We assume that you came across the Blood in your travels. If Dr. Avery wanted you then you are the key. Since you have given us your word that you will return the Blood to its rightful home we will trust in that, within reason of course. We will accompany you to wherever you have it hidden, just as a precaution." The woman sat down next to Tess with a very engaging smile firmly planted on her lovely face. Tess had never had a threat delivered so gently. The U.S. government could learn a thing or two from the Indian intelligence community.

From what she could discern, it seemed to Tess that the Indian agents believed she had somehow stumbled upon the Flame during her travels. If that were the case, then the Sisterhood was protected. She had to quickly come up with a plausible story. She frantically cobbled together a mad hatter's jigsaw puzzle of lies and half-truths.

"I won't dispute anything you have stated. I found the Blood in Romania last summer. I was researching Vlad Tepes, or Vlad the Impaler, you probably know him as Dracula. I had traveled to Transylvania in the Carpathian Mountains just for fun and I ended up in the tent of a Romani fortune-teller. She was in the middle of spinning some crazy story about my future husband when the local police raided the camp. She grabbed the Blood off the center of the table, shoved it in my hands and told me to guard it with my life. I hid it in my backpack just as the police stormed in and arrested her." Tess looked at the four faces to see if they were buying this outrageous fabrication. They seemed riveted.

"The police explained in halting English that I was free to go. I went back to my hotel, packed up and grabbed the first train I could find. I eventually made my way back to England and simply mailed the Blood home from a rural post office. I hadn't any idea what it was until Dr. Avery and his gang kidnapped me. I would be happy to have all of you come with me back to my ranch and I will gladly hand it over. It has caused me enough trouble." Tess tried to look trustworthy and relieved. She was really just buying time. By now the Sisterhood had located her and they would be assembling outside deciding how to safely extricate her from the warehouse.

"We are most grateful for your cooperation Dr. Rankin. Please don't be offended if I express my utter disbelief regarding your fanciful tale. We know that you were in Transylvania last summer and then you traveled on to England, other than that, I don't believe a word of your story." The woman, who appeared to be the leader, held up her hand as Tess began to protest her innocence.

"As I have previously stated, I don't care where you obtained the Blood, it has been lost too us for centuries and now we want it back. We will take you to your ranch and then be on our way." As the woman finished speaking a blinding light flashed across the warehouse and Tess jumped up from the couch, knocked down the nearest agent in front of her and then hit the ground as several warning shots pierced the ceiling; searing pain from her bear wound shot through her leg.

"Place your weapons on the ground in front of you and step away from Dr. Rankin." A forceful voice echoed through the large open space. Considering what had happened to her in the previous days, this was one Russian accent that Tess was happy to hear. Crystal Volkov was their most effective and aggressive Flame Thrower; in Russian her last name meant "wolf", which was particularly apt. She stood like a warrior goddess in a circle of light beams that emanated from the bullet holes in the ceiling.

She was six feet with flaming red hair and a demeanor that intimidated everyone in her wake. Crystal reminded Tess of the famous Celtic Queen Boudicca who led a revolt against the Roman occupation of the British Isles. Tess loved to view the massive bronze statue of Boudicca at the north end of Westminster Bridge in London. Crystal's mother was an American diplomat and her father was a Russian composer, they had lived in Moscow until Crystal joined the U.S. Army when she turned eighteen. Her favorite band was Pussy Riot; that pretty much explained it all.

Crystal remained eerily still as Tess remembered the first time she had encountered her savior. Tess and Liz had been assigned to spend a summer protecting over one hundred women and children in a small refugee camp on the border between Syria and Iraq. One horrific night a group of bandits had attempted to overrun the camp. Crystal rode in on a horse, sprayed the men with automatic weapon fire and they had scattered like cockroaches. Tess had been in awe of her ever after. She was gratified to see that the Sisterhood had sent the most effective weapon in their retrieval arsenal.

In quick order three of the Indians threw down their weapons, dropped to their knees and put their hands behind their heads. Not the woman in charge, she grabbed Tess, pulled her to a standing position in front of her and leveled her gun at Tess' temple. Then she answered Crystal's demand.

"I think not, my fearsome friend. You may drop your weapon and we will walk out of here with Dr. Rankin; we have unfinished business too attend to." She paused while Crystal kept the light shining harshly into their eyes.

"You are not going to shoot Tess." Crystal answered scornfully. "Especially not in front of agents of the United States of America."

The leader called Crystal's bluff. "In less I am mistaken, and I'm not usually incorrect about these things, that is not an American accent. If you do not drop your weapon I will shoot Dr. Rankin in the leg and she will still be of use to us. You choose."

The situation was rapidly spinning out of control. Tess' mind raced with various scenarios regarding how to end the standoff. Most of them concluded with someone injured or possibly dead. She kept reminding herself that the Indian agents were simply doing their jobs and therefore must not be hurt.

"Wait, wait, wait a second here ladies! Since you are talking about me I would like to have a say in this." Tess raised her hands as if to indicate a proposal of a truce. With lightening fast speed she knocked the gun held at her head up in the air, head butted the woman behind her and dove for cover behind Crystal. Tess felt a stream of blood begin to release from her wound.

Crystal leveled her gun at the leader as the woman tried to stem the flow of blood from her nose. With red stained hands, she reluctantly sunk to the floor and assumed the traditional "I surrender" position, as Crystal pulled out a knife and cut the tape from Tess' ankles and wrists. Tess gingerly stepped toward the leader of the group and spoke.

"I am so sorry about your nose." Tess pulled the woman up, tore off material from her own sleeve and attempted to stem the bleeding. She locked eyes with the agent. "I swear that I will give the Indian government back the Blood. It will take a couple of weeks to retrieve it, however, you have my word of honor that I will return it to its rightful country."

The woman spoke directly to Tess. "Oddly enough, I believe you. Quite aside from that, I seem to be out of options. Promise me that when you have the Blood you will bring it to the nearest Indian embassy and alert the media at the same time. My government has already prepared a cover story that does not include any names. Whoever you may be, you are formidable warriors and you have my eternal respect. Go in peace my friend." With that proclamation the leader gathered her troops and headed out of the warehouse. After a few minutes Tess heard the crunch of gravel as the car departed.

With the immediate threat over, Crystal dropped onto the couch and began to laugh so hard she was sputtering. "Damn Tess, you are the craziest woman I have ever met." She spoke in a faux American accent mocking Tess. "I went to Transylvania to study Dracula and I accidentally met a gypsy fortune teller who used the world's largest ruby as her crystal ball. Gee, golly, wiz, I'll do anything to help." Crystal continued to chuckle as Tess joined her on the couch, wincing in pain.

Because Crystal was acting goofy Tess immediately relaxed and finally let her guard down. "Look smart ass, with everything I have been through in the last few days you're lucky I don't smack you silly. I am too tired to try. And the correct term is Romani not gypsy; that is why people should not use the term 'gipped', it is a racial slur. So what next?" Tess looked around at the abandoned warehouse.

Crystal chuckled, slapped Tess on the back and reached out a hand to haul her up. "I am wearing a wire so our car should be here any minute. I approached on foot from down the road; you know 'the element of surprise' and all that. Let's get you out into some fresh air and fix that leg, by the by, props for tangling with a Grizzly and living to tell the story. Just so you know, I grabbed your bag from their car before I came in."

Tess and Crystal made their way out of the warehouse just as a massive black SUV pulled up and Weston jumped out from the driver's side. He moved swiftly and gracefully for such a huge man. He swept Tess up in a bearlike embrace. "We have been worried about you little sis. In fact, I haven't had much sleep the last few days with picking up Deb and getting her back home, then returning to retrieve your silly bones."

Since the day that Leigh-Anne had fallen in love with Weston he had become part of the Sisterhood. He referred to all of the younger women as "Little Sis" and all of the younger men as "Bro" but the way he pronounced Bro it sounded like "Bra". He called older men and women, such as Nana and Papa, "Auntie" and "Uncle".

Tess was not sure if this was a typical Maori tradition or something that just came from Weston's family. Either way, she loved it. Weston made everyone feel as if they were all a members of the same tribe. She gave him one last heartfelt squeeze as she climbed into the front seat.

"Okay, the band is back together, where the heck is everyone else? I assume that you had more than just the two of you on this adventure." Tess looked back and forth between Weston in the driver's seat and Crystal in the back.

Crystal spoke. "Yep, we sent everyone else off on various assignments. The three of us are heading back to Queenstown. We need to meet with Liz and Weston's true luuuuuuuv." Crystal teased Weston as he in turn rolled his eyes and chuckled. "With all of this activity around you and the Flame we have to rework the security measures for your dive with Deb."

Tess jumped as Deb's name was mentioned. "Wait, so Deb is in New Zealand? I guess she opened the safety deposit box. But Deb is not certified for a deep dive."

Weston chimed in. "No worries, you will train her when you get to Queenstown. She is farther along with her diving experience than anyone at headquarters and she's your best friend. You have to wait a couple of weeks for the lake to lower anyway. That will give you plenty of time. Now let's get going. We figured that we couldn't leave the jet at Helena Regional Airport because U.S. agents will be all over that place. We will drive down into Wyoming and fly out of the Casper/Natrona County International Airport."

Tess leaned her head back against the seat. She had been surviving on adrenalin for so many days that she was dizzy with exhaustion. Turning herself over to the more than capable hands of Weston and Crystal was a relief.

She absentmindedly rubbed her cross necklace. All female members of the Sisterhood were presented with a silver cross necklace at their induction ceremony. The cross had a rose wrapped around it to symbolize the sacred Yellow Rose.

Tess had been told by Nana that the Yellow Rose Cross was designed by Alice Paul and Sara when they began the Sisterhood of the Yellow Rose after the 19th Amendment was ratified. Paul, Susan B. Anthony and Lucretia Mott were all Quakers and there had always been a religious element to the women's rights movement in the U.S., the Seneca Falls Convention had been held in the Wesleyan Methodist Church that was built by a congregation of abolitionists.

Sara was Lutheran, Lucy Burns had been a devout Catholic and many of the Suffragists were deeply religious men and women, therefore the Yellow Rose Cross was a natural symbol for the Sisterhood. As Tess continued to caress her good luck charm she contemplated the involvement of so many actors in this dangerous play. A dark feeling of foreboding settled upon her as the full realization of her precarious position sunk in.

Too many countries. Too many agents. Too many loyalties. Too much money. Someone was bound to find her. It was just a matter of time.

CHAPTER SIXTEEN

"We found something!" Robyn and Mason were out of breath as they jumped from the front seat of Mason's pickup and raced toward Jack and Gregg sitting on the porch of Tess' home, drinking coffee surrounded by heat lamps. There had been several snow falls, as was expected for late November, however, the last few days had been unseasonably mild. Thor was sprawled out next to Jack's feet.

"Hold up you two, settle down and join us. We have been at this for over a week. What has got you so fired up all of a sudden?" Gregg leaned toward the two deputies as they sat down in rocking chairs facing the men.

"Okay, well first off, we found a connection between two of the main airports we have been watching." Robyn was gulping air. "For days now we have been going through hours and hours of footage that Sheriff Mike got from his buddy at the CIA. We have been focusing on three airports: LAX, Helena and Casper. Today we hit pay dirt!"

Mason spoke up as Robyn pulled a laptop from her bag. "We recognized someone. Gregg, remember that big fella you pointed out to us a few days back when we first got the footage from LAX?" Mason paused as Gregg nodded.

"Well, danged if we didn't find him again! Right here at the Casper airport!" Jack and Gregg jumped at the first solid lead they had had in days.

"Wait, are you saying you have him in custody?" Jack attempted to rise as Mason placed his hand on Jack's shoulder.

"Nope, settle your hash a minute cowboy. We found footage of him getting on a private plane with two passengers. One was a smokin' redhead that I would give my left nut, sorry for the language Robyn, to meet and the other was all covered up. We thought Gregg could do his Native American mojo thingy and tell us if it was Tess from the way she walked." Mason stopped to take a breath as Robyn flipped open the computer and brought up the video file.

"Here is the first footage that Gregg identified. See the big guy that Gregg pointed out. Now I'm going to split the screen . . ." Robyn hurriedly pressed several keys as a second window opened, ". . . and lookie here. It's the same guy! Now Gregg and Jack, tell me if this third person is Tess." Robyn pointed to a figure on the screen and waited for the men to watch both of the videos as they repeated on an endless loop.

"It's Tess!" Gregg and Jack chimed in at the same moment. Jack pressed on. "So where did they go? Did you get the flight plan from the Casper airport?"

"Here's where is gets weird." Mason sheepishly looked at the two men before he delivered his news. "Robyn and I went to the Casper airport and spoke to the head traffic controller. He insists that it is impossible for a plane to take off without an approved flight plan. In fact it would be suicide. Planes would be running into each other. The problem is that he couldn't locate the flight plan. He said that it had been wiped from every system they have. He agreed to get their best programmers on it, but for now it seems to have vanished."

Jack exploded. "What in the hell! This two bit . . ." He jumped up and began pacing the porch, all the while muttering indecipherable curses. Oddly enough, Gregg was eerily calm as he watched the videos over and over. Then he spoke.

"Robyn could you email me this file? I want to study it a little more. Right now Jack and I have plans to meet with the new recruits from the reservation. The young men and women that come and work at the Double R over the holidays need to be trained." Gregg stood up, handed Robyn her computer and slapped Mason on the back. "Thanks for showing that to us. We will get right on it after our meeting." He tipped his Stetson and walked into the house as the other three stood on the porch looking perplexed.

Jack filled in the silence. "Really, thanks so much you two. All of you are doing a great job with very little to go on. If Gregg or I come up with anything substantial we will call you right away." Jack watched as Robyn emailed the file to Gregg. Mason and Robyn gave Jack one last bewildered look as they got into the truck and drove away. Jack turned off all the porch heaters and walked inside. He found Gregg in the library on the computer frantically hitting keys.

"What happened out there? First off you were just plain rude to Mason and Robyn, then you were acting as if we have not been working day and night to find Tess and Deb. I can't remember when I last slept. We have been living on adrenalin and coffee for days!" Jack walked over to Gregg and looked at the computer screen. An incredulous grin broke over his exhausted features.

"Holy hell, that's him!!! How? Where? What led you to?" Jack couldn't complete a sentence. He was looking at a picture of the same man from LAX and Casper.

Gregg swung the desk chair around and looked in triumph at Jack. "Let me ask you something my intrepid friend.

Which country consistently fields the reigning world champions in both men and women's rugby? Coincidentally, which country was the first to grant women universal suffrage?"

"New Zealand!!! They are in New Zealand!!!" Jack and Gregg did a complicated bro hug fist bump combination that only males could replicate.

"Yes, we are looking at Weston Maaka. Maaka is Maori for Mark; which was the God of War. Maaka was one of the most ferocious rugby players that ever stalked the ground. I thought I recognized him, but I just could not place him. Then when I saw the way he walked through the Casper airport it hit me." Gregg swiveled his chair back to point at the screen as Jack looked at dozens of pictures of Maaka.

"Rugby was first introduced to New Zealand in 1870 by Charles Monro. It quickly grew to become the national sport. Maaka was on the national team, which I am sure you remember is called the All Blacks because they wear black uniforms. The All Blacks team is a selection of the best Maori rugby players in New Zealand. I am sure you have seen them perform their intimidating ritual Haka, which generally scares the bejesus out of the opposing team. So New Zealand it is my friend." Gregg smiled triumphantly at a grinning Jack.

"Okay, so now what? I just go to New Zealand and wander around each of the main cities? That could take weeks." Jack began pacing the library floor.

"No, that won't work. First we need to throw everyone off the track. I will stay here and you book a flight to Australia, I know it's close but that is the best we can do. When you get there you need to somehow arrange to fly or sail to New Zealand without anyone knowing. Do you think you could manage that?" Gregg looked at Jack.

Jack stopped pacing as a wild grin broke out on his previously pensive face. "I can do that! I have a grad school friend who lives in Sydney and she teaches the history of the Americas. I could contact my parents and tell them that Missy agreed to help me with research. It's pretty thin, but they might buy it."

As Gregg switched to a ticket booking site, Jack contemplated how to handle his parents and President Thomson. He knew that no matter where he went government agents would follow. He was absolutely sure that his parents had figured out by now that he was in Wyoming at the Double R. Because the website stated that he needed an entry visa and he would have to use his passport, there would be no way to hide the Australia trip. It was better to act as if he were desperately jumping around trying to find help, than to seem more organized and calculating.

Jack raced up the stairs two at a time as Thor began to bark excitedly. He had been sleeping in Tess' room with Thor by his side. Now he ran around and randomly threw items of clothing into his bag. It was summer in Australia and New Zealand so he would just have to buy more clothes when he got there. He quickly called Missy, hang the time difference, and woke her up. He gave her only the briefest of explanations and then rang off.

Jack stopped for a moment and looked out the window. He could feel Tess. It had nothing to do with being in her room. He could sense himself getting closer to her. It was an odd sensation that he had never experienced before. It was dangerous, it was foolhardy and it was stupidly crazy. Some gravitational pull was inexorably drawing him to her. So, finally, this was love.

CHAPTER SEVENTEEN

President Thomson contemplated the beauty of the suffrage sculpture. The Carrara marble gleamed a ghostly white in the moonlit Capitol Rotunda. The NWP had presented the, Portrait Monument to Lucretia Mott, Elizabeth Cady Stanton and Susan B. Anthony, to the U.S., in February of 1921. Created by Adelaide Johnson it had featured the inscription, "Woman, first denied a soul, then called mindless, now arisen, declared herself an entity to be reckoned."

She was ever mindful that because of the efforts of tens of thousands of women and men, during the seventy-two year fight for suffrage, she now resided in the White House. She was not the first woman president, nor would she be the last, however, the burden of smashing through that last great glass ceiling had cost her dearly.

Friendships left to wither due to lack of time, sibling's birthdays missed or forgotten, children's and grandchildren's plays and soccer games unattended. If it had not been for Rob, she would have never had a life outside of the political spectrum. Rob was as beautiful and solid as the sculpture before her.

"Interesting place to meet." Nancy Avery walked up to join President Thomson. "So are we getting maudlin?" Nancy gently nudged her friend's shoulder with her own.

"Not maudlin, just contemplative. I'm thinking back over the years about friendships lost and power gained." President Thomson stepped out of her misty memories and looked at Nancy. They had been best friends since kindergarten. Through life's ups and downs, she and Nancy had clung together. When she and Rob had gotten pregnant in college, Nancy had stood beside her and helped her through graduation and law school. Nancy had been their babysitter, counselor and stalwart friend. It was time to return the favor. "So where in the world is your errant progeny?" She asked with a smile.

"Australia. His cover story is visiting a friend from grad school, who may be able to help him track down information on the secret location of the Sisterhood. Obviously, he discovered New Zealand. So what's the plan here? Do we just let him make his way there and see how this plays out?" Nancy asked.

"We decided that we have to pretend we don't know anything about the Sisterhood. Let's stick with that. For my part it is true. I am not a member and I only know what you have shared with me. I assume you have contacted the rest of the board. What do they suggest?" President Thomson turned to look at her dearest friend.

"We agreed on a 'wait and see' position. Tess and Deb are practicing their deep dives and will be ready to go in two weeks when the lake lowers. Jack will make his way to New Zealand and I assume he will figure out they are in Queenstown. He seems to be drawn to Tess like a planet circling the sun." Nancy's face showed a worried grimace.

"You can't stop true love Nancy. You just have to accept it."

"I know, but he will be with a woman who puts her life in danger . . ."

"In danger for a good cause." President Thomson reminded her.

". . . sure, in danger for a good cause. My grandchildren could end up being motherless during any given summer. It is such a precarious life." Nancy shook her head as if to dispel further terrifying images.

"That is the life Jack has chosen. You even tired to scare him with the Flame Thrower information and look what happened. He raced off to Wyoming and clued in the entire sheriff's department. We have to contain this spread. I trust that Sheriff Mike, Edward, Robyn, Mason and Gregg will keep Tess' associations to themselves. With the exception of Gregg, who seems devoted to Tess' family, they are all law enforcement officers. They would not do anything to endanger Deb or Tess." President Thomson looked to Nancy for confirmation.

"I suppose you are right, as always. Sheriff Mike's CIA buddy and Agent Howard of the FBI have been very helpful with the feeding of information to the folks in Wyoming. Apparently it has paid off. Somehow Jack and Gregg figured out Tess' location. So it is agreed. We'll let Jack find his way to Tess if he can." Nancy turned to study the sculpture. "It's exquisite, Adelaide Johnson was truly gifted. What do you think those ladies would make of us?"

"Mott, Cady Stanton and Anthony were pretty fierce. I suppose they would tell us to do what is right and somehow protect the Sisterhood."

"So you have decided to turn the Flame over to the Indian government?" Nancy asked.

"Yes, it is the right thing to do. It has raised the profile of the Sisterhood. I may not be a member, but I am a woman and the Sisterhood's work must be allowed to continue unabated. I'm not sure how to bring this up, so I will just tell you about the security measures I put in place. I have called in the Naval Special Warfare Development Group. They will set up on Hidden Island the night before the dive. Their orders are to secure the lake area and engage only if Tess and Deb are in danger . . ." President Thomson was interrupted by Nancy.

"Wait, what the hell! You are talking about SEAL Team 6, the special-forces group that killed Osama bin Laden. I thought they were disbanded after August 6, 2011 when thirty-eight people died, including seventeen SEAL's, in Afghanistan, in what was widely reported to be a revenge killing for the hit on bin Laden. Why? Why are you sending them in?" Nancy could not contain her distress as she focused her eyes on her life long friend.

President Thomson help up her hands. "Wait, just let me finish before you meltdown. Everything you have said is true, they are SEAL Team 6, they were not disbanded. We must have these groups of highly trained men and women to handle situations such as this. I am well aware of the Sisterhood's prowess when it comes to self-defense. You have explained all about the training of the Flame Throwers. I assume that when Deb and Tess do their dive the persons left on the boat will be the most lethal agents the Sisterhood has." Nancy anxiously shifted her weight as President Thomson continued.

"However, we are dealing with forces beyond our control. The Russians are experts at this sort of mission and they want the Flame. The British Special Forces are the finest in the world and they are hot on the trail. So far, we have not picked up any information on the Brazilians or the Portuguese hunting for the Flame. To be fair, all of those countries have a legitimate claim to the jewel." President Thomson paused as Nancy nodded her head in agreement.

"So we have chosen to give it back to India. It is theirs by history and right. Don't you agree?" She paused as Nancy finally spoke.

"Yes, yes, I agree that we must return the Flame or the Blood or whatever you want to call it to India. I just simply don't understand why you think we need the additional fire-power of SEAL Team 6. Surely the Russians, Brits and anyone else claiming the Flame would not have the nerve to attack Deb and Tess." Nancy turned anxious eyes toward her friend.

"Nancy, the Sisterhood is not a U.S. governmental agency. Any of the entities that I mentioned would use force, if not deadly force to get the Flame back. They all share the belief that the Flame belongs to their country. Whether they know about, or suspect, the existence of a secret organization, they will do their best to track it down. They don't care if it is an individual or a group. They would only pause if our government had possession of the Flame."

"But SEAL Team 6 is an assassination team! I'm going to contact Jack and get him out of there!" Nancy frantically searched through her briefcase as President Thomson laid her hand on Nancy's arm.

"You will do no such thing. If Jack is being followed, and he actually gets to Queenstown, our team will protect him. SEAL Team 6 is also an extraction team. It is the only way for us to know which other countries are on the trail of the Flame."

"Wait, are you saying that you intend to use my son as bait to lure out dangerous agents from other countries, because if that is true we are done!" Nancy locked furious eyes on her friend.

"No, Nan, that is not what I am doing! I love Jack; I'm trying to protect him! Whether you like it or not, your son has fallen in love with a Flame Thrower, that makes his life more dangerous. That is his choice. I am sending the team out with two orders. First and foremost they will protect Jack, Tess and anyone else that is involved with the Flame, secondly, they will retrieve the Flame from the Sisterhood and we will return it to the Indian government. Please don't think I would ever use him as a pawn. He is like my own son." President Thomson wrapped her arms around Nancy.

Nancy relaxed into the embrace of her dearest friend. It was all true, Jack had chosen his destiny and she had to accept and respect his decision. She straightened up and pulled her arm through her friend's.

As two of the most powerful women in the world studied the gleaming sculpture, clouds swept across the full moon, sending a darkening shroud around the ethereally white surface of the Suffragists' faces.

The mission had to continue. Women and children around the world had to be protected. The Sisterhood's secrets and finances must be guarded. Nancy stood beside her best friend and considered the intricate web of lies that she had woven. Secrets kept from her colleagues, friends, husband and children, all in the name of the Sisterhood.

It was a torturous form of irony that her own son had fallen in love with a Flame Thrower. So be it. She would work with the president, SEAL Team 6 or any other entity that could ensure Jack's safety. In a few weeks, when all of this was finished, she would try to reason with Jack. If that didn't work, she had other avenues at her disposal. Either way Jack and Tess would be over.

CHAPTER EIGHTEEN

Jack looked at his friend Missy. She was tall, about five-nine, blonde and beautiful. He thought back to their time together in grad school wondering why they had never become a couple. Then it hit him, because she scared the crap out of him. He never knew what she would do next.

He recalled the first time he met her. She had brazenly walked up to him waiting outside a classroom and said, "You have to drop this class, she is bat poop crazy," in an Oklahoman twang. Then she led him to the admin building and helped him drop the class and add another class that she was taking.

Missy then took him out to lunch and told him all about her life in Lane, Oklahoma, which was in Atoka County not far from the Texas border. She had attended Atoka High because Lane's population stood at around five hundred souls. She had gone on to Eastern Oklahoma State where she had majored in history and was on the dance team that evolved into Pom Pom girls for the basketball team. The school mascot was the

Mountaineers, although that was confusing because Jack had never seen any mountains in Oklahoma.

Missy was a force of nature that occasionally had to bring her students to what she called, "Come to Jesus," moments in class when they got out of hand. He knew that over the years her students both feared and worshipped her. She had just finished wrapping up the semester before the holiday break when he arrived.

Luckily for him, she immediately volunteered to accompany him on his adventure. She had a friend who was the captain of a freighter and he smuggled them aboard when his ship left Sydney. They were now slowly making their way to Auckland.

"So I said to my daddy, 'Daddy, Lane Baptist Church is lucky to have you and your brother playing guitar and if they don't let you play the songs you want they can hang from the highest tree,' but he didn't feel like that was the Christian way to handle it . . ." Missy poked Jack in the shoulder, " . . .hey, are you listening? You look about a million miles away."

Jack shook himself out of the past. "Sorry, you were telling some homey story about Lane Baptist Church. Wait didn't you say Reba McEntire went to church with you?"

"No, dang Jack, you don't listen to a word I say. Reba McEntire came from our area; one of her relatives went to our church. I was telling you about daddy wanting to play the Wampus Cat's fight song in church and the preacher gettin' all heapt up about it." Missy paused as Jack respectfully raised his hand to speak.

"Point of order judge, what in the tar nation is a Wampus Cat?"

"Jack don't make fun of how we speak, we don't use tar nation; we aren't a bunch of hillbillies. For your information my mama speaks three languages. Now where was I? Right, the Wampus Cat is the mascot for Atoka High, it is some kind of Cherokee mythological half-woman, half-cougar thingy, anyway that's not the point, I told my daddy that since he is playing for free he should play whatever the hell, excuse my language, he wants." Missy ran out of steam as a knock echoed through their metal cabin.

Bert Smith, the captain of the freighter, poked his head in. "Missy, Jack, something strange is going on here." He entered their cabin, grabbed a chair and sat down. "I just spoke with my first mate and he thinks someone else was smuggled on board. Now this is a huge ship and it could have been easily done, as evidenced by you two. One of my sailors is acting a bit cagey and he has been flashing a wad of cash around when the men play poker. The first mate said that some food was missing from the galley and he found wrappers near a storage unit."

"Wait, so you think this other person on board has something to do with us?" Jack stood up and began to rummage through his clothing for his hunting knife. "If that is true we need to find out right away. I don't want Missy in any danger."

"Now hold up Jack, don't go off half cocked. It could be anyone. Maybe even a kid running away from home. What do you intend to do Bert?" Missy enquired of the captain.

"Just stay here. I am going to take a couple of men and do a complete deck-by- deck sweep. Lock your door and don't open it until I come back to check on you." Bert stood up and walked out.

"Oh, man this is bad, bad and all kinds of bad Jack. If anyone gets hurt because Bert did me a favor I'll never forgive myself." Missy began to pace back and forth in their small cabin.

"Listen Missy, I'm sure it's nothing. Maybe even rats, this ship must be loaded with them. Let's just wait here until Bert gets back. We have been at sea for over a week; if anyone were after us they would have made a move by now." Jack sat down on the chair that Bert had vacated.

"I don't know Jack. I've got a weird feeling. You know that gut instinct thing when you are absolutely sure you are being watched? Well, I have had it since we got on this ship. I just shrugged it off and figured that it was because I am the only woman aboard. Now I don't know. My survival alarms bells are shrieking like our tornado-warning siren at the Lane volunteer fire station." Missy plopped down on one of the bunks.

"Look Missy, just breathe. Bert will be back and we can go out on deck to enjoy the wind or throw up, whichever happens first." Just as Jack finished speaking a loud knock reverberated through the cabin. "See I told you." Jack swung the door open as Missy yelled.

"No Jack, don't, that's not Bert this soon." Her voice trailed off as a gun wielding man rushed in and slammed the door all in one fluid motion. The soft "click," of the inside lock sealed their fate.

"Alright, let's just keep our heads about us and no one gets hurt. Jack, sit down on the chair. Melissa stay where you are." The unknown assailant watched as Jack retreated into the back of the cabin and sat down, warily eyeing the intruder. "Thanks for your cooperation. Now it seems the captain and his mates are looking for me, so I better be brief. You have information I want and if you don't come with me I will shoot Melissa." With that declaration the man leveled the gun at Missy's head.

"Wait, wait! No need for that. I assume you are speaking about the location of the Flame." When the man nodded Jack continued, "It is in Auckland, we hopped a freighter so that we could get past customs. I will take you to the exact location. Please don't hurt her."

Jack was desperately trying to place the accent of the gunman, it sounded like a romance language dialect with a hint of Eastern Europe, then it hit him, it was Portuguese! Of course, he remembered that when he had first gone to Portugal one of his friends had said jokingly, that the Portuguese language sounded like a drunk Russian trying to speak Spanish, it was the perfect description. Great, this was the last thing they needed.

The gunman might be some sort of agent of the Portuguese government, or he was a freelancer, either way, Jack had to protect Missy and get this guy out of the cabin. How long before Bert's return? Jack hoped it would be soon. He had to keep the guy talking.

"Look." Jack held up his hands and tried to appear frightened, it wasn't a stretch. "I want to get you out of this cabin, so just tell me how you see this playing out." It was always best to give the person holding the gun a show of respect.

"I appreciate that Jack. Since I have no reason to trust you I will be taking you with me. Melissa, would you please tape Jack's hands?" The gunman reached into his jacket pocket, pulled out a roll of duck tape and handed it to Missy. "Now let's all stay nice and calm. Melissa don't make any sudden moves and we will be out of here soon enough. There are several life boats on board and we will procure one."

Missy's hands were shaking as she took the roll, walked behind Jack's chair and began to wrap the tape loosely around Jack's wrists. She hoped that perhaps Jack could wiggle one hand out eventually.

"Let's not be so easy with the restraints Melissa. Wrap it good and tight or I will have to teach you a lesson." The gunman pointed his weapon at Missy's knee. "I would hate to ruin those lovely long legs."

Jack could feel a cold trickle of sweat run down his back as Missy cinched the tape tighter. Her breath was coming in short spurts across his hair. She was terrified, and this was a woman who used to shoot rattlesnakes for a buck each for her dad. He had to do something. If he could somehow get Missy to stay behind him, maybe he could body slam the man against the door.

His mind was a wild kaleidoscope of various scenarios, all of which ended badly. Rushing headlong into the guy was out of the question. If the gun went off in the small metal cabin it could ricochet anywhere. Where in the hell was Bert?

Missy finished taping Jack and obediently sat back down on the bunk. She had a crazy look in her eye and she seemed to be making some sort of decision. Oh no! The Oklahoman, wild west, shoot first and ask questions later, part of her upbringing had kicked in. Who knew what she was planning. Jack had to get the guy out of the cabin before Missy had a chance to act on her unquestionably ill-conceived plot.

"Okay, I've just been hog-tied by a professional." This earned Jack a smirk from Missy. "I am ready to go." Jack stood up and began to take a step toward the man, as Missy lunged for the gun. A shot rang out as Missy wrestled with the man like a deranged welterweight.

Jack was knocked back against the far wall as he tried to rush the gunman. Adrenalin raced through him while he attempted to right himself. Rhythmic pounding on the door announced that Bert and his men had returned.

Jack could hear shouting and what sounded like a scraping sound; he assumed that Bert was desperately trying to unlock the door. Another shot reverberated through the small cabin as Missy managed to pull the door open. Men rushed in from the outside, grabbed the gunman and forced him to the ground.

Missy turned and rushed toward Jack as he slumped to the ground. A searing pain burned its way across his left side. "I think he got me, partner."

"Jack, don't even joke about that." Missy looked on in horror as a quick flowing spring of blood spread across Jack's chest. "Oh no! Oh baby Jesus! Jack! Wait hang on! Bert, Jack's been shot!"

Time seemed to slow as Jack watched the men lift his body and rush him to the infirmary. The ship's doctor hooked him up to an IV as Missy and Bert scurried around yelling orders. Oddly enough, there was no sound and no pain; just a swirling pool of quiet reflection amid the outside chaos.

He was not even afraid. He grabbed Missy's arm and whispered, "Tell Tess I love her." He had just enough time to register that a fatal amount of blood flow was coming from his body before everything went black.

CHAPTER NINETEEN

"Hey lazy butt, get off the couch and come for a run."
Liz kicked the side of the couch as Tess attempted to ignore
her. "You need to get out in the fresh air. I know you have
been fighting off the flu, but the sunshine will do you some
good, now hoist your sorry carcass up. Your leg has healed
nicely and you will do the 'big-dive' in two days. Everything is
going smoothly and according to plan."

"Alright, stop nagging me. Man, I rest for one second
and you turn into a drill sergeant. I don't feel peppy; is that a
crime? Being here is messing with my Christmas buzz. I don't
want it to be hot; I want snow, hot cocoa and blazing fires.
This is wrong." Tess swung her legs over the side of the
couch, rose and walked toward the large windows.

"Look, I know that's not what is going on here; you are
pining for that hunk of burnin' love back in the U.S.. If it makes
you feel any better you can race back to him and that frozen
tundra you call a state as soon as you are cleared to fly.
Leigh-Anne said that you could finally bring Nana and Papa
home. So all of you will be snug as bugs in rugs a few days

before Christmas. Now stop whining and go change." Liz patted her dearest friend on the shoulder.

Tess mumbled something about a "forced march," and went off to change. Liz was putting up a brave front. She was actually very worried about Tess. She seemed to lack focus and several times had not been able to complete the dive training for Deb.

The Sisterhood had found another woman to do some deep dives with Deb in order to get her ready. Tess had been down with the flu and now she seemed constantly depressed. In fact, Liz had never seen her friend like this, even in the dark days of her recovery after their attack.

Tess, Nana and Papa were the royal family of the Sisterhood; they were the last links to the beginning of their organization. Liz was determined to see Tess through to the end of her mission. The board had agreed to give the Indian government the Flame and everyone had decided that it was for the best. The Rankin family, the board, Leigh-Anne and Liz were the only persons that knew about the Sparks.

The Sparks were smaller companion pieces to the Flame. There were fourteen rubies in all. Each of the rubies were worth roughly a million dollars and over the years they had been sold off to raise cash. The Sisterhood still had eight

Sparks, along with dozens of precious gems that had been in the satchel when Sara escaped from England.

No one outside of their small group knew of the existence of the treasure trove that kept the Sisterhood solvent and secret. Liz took heart in the fact that in every exchange and recording, not one single person mentioned the Sparks or the rest of the hoard that had been on the ill-fated train.

Of course there was always a wild card and that was Jack. Whether she admitted it or not, Tess was in love with him. Liz should have been happy that her best friend had finally found a person the share her life with, however, she could not shake off the feeling that Jack brought extreme danger to their organization.

Nancy had tried to contain her son, but it was too late. He had fallen off the grid and they could only assume that he was somehow making his way to New Zealand. Liz and Leigh-Anne had decided to keep Tess out of the loop when it came to surveillance of Jack. Considering Tess' lethargic state, they might have to reconsider.

Tess returned with a bit of a bounce in her step. "Alright, I will stop moping around and go for a run. I am suddenly famished." She ran outside and began to warm up on the lawn overlooking the lake.

Liz smiled at the use of the word "famished." The entire Sisterhood had not used the word "starving," for decades. Each of the Flame Throwers spent most of their time with people who were really starving. People meant they were hungry or famished, not starving: every aid worker they had encountered had pressed this point. Words have power; they should not be used lightly.

Liz joined Tess in her warm-up and then they headed around the lake towards town. Liz still marveled at the other-world beauty of Queenstown. Between the snow-capped towering mountains and the crystal blue lake, it was one of the most stunning places she had ever seen.

Queenstown advertised itself as the, "Adventure Capital of the World," and it did have a point. There were over two-hundred adventure tourist activities to do in the small town and surrounding area. A.J. Hackett had created the world's first organized and permanent bungy jump off the suspension bridge over the Kawarau Gorge.

The town was also a world-class leader in: skiing (including glacier skiing), rafting, skydiving, river-surfing and jet boating. Liz had gone jet boating on the Shotover River one time. The boat had careened wildly through narrow canyons and then done several 360 degree spins, which ended in her nearly retching into the icy water.

Wollstonecraft House had been created to match the dramatic beauty of Queenstown. With its massive windows, ivy covered brick walls and rounded turrets, it looked like a modern castle. What the locals did not see were the subterranean levels.

In the early nineties, it became apparent that with the onset of the computer age the Sisterhood needed to turn an antiquated basement into a communications nerve center. Workers had been brought in from out of the country while the house was sealed off for a year. Two floors were added below the building and their tech department was created. Now they had over a dozen women working in the IT department. Alex and Theo were their first male hires. The Sisterhood could not ignore their exceptional skills and willingness to relocate; so far, they were working out splendidly.

"Let's run up Stanley Street to Shotover Street and stop at Fergburger." Tess was beginning to feel a good deal better. She had been in a funk since her arrival. It was very disconcerting considering the fact that she prided herself on always being upbeat and assertive. She decided that she would shake off her lethargy and throw herself into the task at hand. She and Deb would need all of their concentration to do the dive and retrieve the Flame.

"You are on, let's race." Liz took off at a blinding speed as Tess struggled to catch up.

"Wait up, you maniac!" Tess stretched out her stride and felt the satisfaction of a full tilt run. They raced past the gaggles of tourists until they reached hollowed ground. As they stood in front of the world famous Fergburger, they bent over and caught their respective breathes.

"I am going to have the Cock Cajun, just because it is fun to say." Liz held the door open for Tess as they both entered the greatest hamburger place on the planet.

"You're such a freak. I'm having the Chief Wiggum and some onion rings. Why don't you grab a table and I'll get our food." Tess walked up to the raised counter and ordered. The entire Sisterhood, along with thousands of people from around the globe, universally agreed that Fergburger served the best burgers anyone had ever sunk their teeth into. It was a magical mix of the bun and meat, along with several homemade secret sauces, that created a carnivore nirvana.

Tess marveled at the varied cuisine Queenstown had to offer; from fabulous Thai to down-home steak and fries, the small town was bursting with five star dining establishments. For breakfast and High Tea, The Dairy hotel was in a class by itself. Matt and Paul had created the most luxurious experience in Queenstown; between the immaculately kept rooms and the sumptuously appointed common areas of the hotel, The Dairy was the undisputed jewel of the town.

Tess joined her friend at a small wooden table. "Sorry about the crummy mood."

"You don't need to apologize . . ." Liz began

"I do." Tess enjoined. "I don't know what is up with me lately."

"It's him, right?"

"Yep." Tess locked eyes with her friend.

"So you what? You have fallen for a guy you just met?"

"Yep."

"And you don't find that a bit strange after everything that we went through?"

"Nope."

"So since we were sixteen you have been terrified of men and now that is okay? Everything is fine with you now that you met Jack? You don't cringe from his advances? You don't jump if he touches you?" Liz looked unbelievingly at her friend.

"Yes. I am finally free. I hope that someday the same thing will happen for you. If we don't heal Dalton wins. Every opportunity we have missed out on for over ten years is a victory for Dalton. He broke us Liz. Now we have to find a way to mend. I chose Jack. I want Jack. I will fight to get Jack back. I am going to live, really live, for the first time since that nightmarish summer. I want the same thing for you." Tess reached across and quickly squeezed Liz's folded hands as the food arrived.

"So in this scenario I am Susan B Anthony, childless and single for the rest of my life and you are Elizabeth Cady Stanton, married and raising seven kids?" Liz looked down at her plate.

"No, that is not at all how I see us in the future. First off, I'm not having seven kids, yeesh!! Elizabeth Cady Stanton was hard-core. She is a role model for all women, however, Susan B Anthony was in the field working night and day for women's suffrage. That is us. You and me. We are the foot soldiers. We will emulate their fifty-year partnership. Hell, we will outlast them by years." Tess abandoned her attempt to cheer up Liz.

The women sat brooding as they hungrily devoured their food. Each of them lost in their tormented remembrances of the brutal attack. Liz was the first to break the silence.

"I want to move forward. I have tried. I just . . . well, I can't seem to bloom. Does that sound confusing? I feel as if I closed up that day, as if I am always a bud waiting to flower, but I lack sunshine or water." Liz looked at her friend for a sign of understanding.

"I know sweetie, of all people I know. I believe that someday it will happen for you, when you are ready. You will look up and out of yourself, gaze across a treacherous space and see someone, really see someone. When that happens you will hold on and never surrender. We are social animals Liz; it's inevitable. I feel that way about Jack . . . wait it's Jack!" Tess jumped up as a tall man entered the restaurant. On one arm he had a cast and on his other arm he had a tall, gorgeous blonde.

"Hello ladies, might we join you. I told my friend Missy that Queenstown was so small that eventually we would run into you." Jack pulled another tiny table close to theirs and sat down. "Missy this is the woman who all the fuss is about, Tess this is Missy my friend from grad school. I assume that you are Liz, nice to finally meet you."

Missy mumbled something that sounded like, "A lot of fuss for a little lady," shook hands with the women and went off to place an order. She stood at the counter warily eyeing the group as if they were a pack of salivating jackals.

Jack continued. "Well, I am having my usual, the Big Al without beetroot and eggs, mainly because I don't know what the hell beetroot is and I'll be damned if I am going to eat eggs on a hamburger. Of all the freaky things to put on . . ." Jack never finished his sentence as Tess jumped up, grabbed him and burst into tears.

CHAPTER TWENTY

"So I simply began to follow house names. I knew that your headquarters in NYC was called the Ida B. Wells House, after the famous African American civil rights pioneer. Don't worry Tess . . ." Jack looked adoringly at the object of his affection. For her part, she seemed mesmerized by his story. "I explained to Missy the courageous background of Ms. Wells, including her anti-lynching campaigns, being thrown off a train for refusing to give up her seat and the 1891 segregated streetcar boycott in Atlanta. Both of the last events remind me of Rosa Parks." He stopped to take a breath.

"I did remember to include the fact that she was a writer and published her own newspaper the Free Speech and a prominent Suffragist. Let's see, where was I? Right, then we noticed that your headquarters in S.F. was called the Lucy Stone House.

Missy remembered that Ms. Stone was the first woman in the U.S. to receive a B.A. and she told me all about her brave work with the abolitionist movement including a story about a protestor throwing a Bible at her head, of all things. As we discussed the fact that Lucy Stone founded the American Woman Suffrage Association and her publishing of the weekly newspaper, The Woman's Journal, it hit us." While Jack paused, Liz hoped that he would finally wrap up his meandering tale of how he found Tess.

"We realized that if Mary Wollstonecraft was considered the 'mother,' of the women's rights movement and the first country to grant women suffrage was New Zealand, then there had to be a Wollstonecraft House here. So we simply put the name in Google and made our way." Jack took an enormous bite of his hamburger as the three women looked on.

"Well, let me just add one little wrinkle, Jack got shot in the arm trying to find you. There is that." Missy glared at Tess with undisguised fury. "Let me repeat myself so we are all clear on this. Jack. Got. Shot! So you had better be worth it or I am going to kick your butt from here to next Sunday."

"Now, now Missy, pull it back and take your finger off the proverbial trigger." Jack patted Missy on the head. At this point Tess seemed to fully absorb what was happening.

"Jack you were shot? How, where, by whom?"

"Don't worry Tess, it's just a flesh wound." Jack smiled his most lethal grin.

"Wait, you can't use a Monty Python line on me and expect to laugh your way out of this. You were shot! Because of me!" Tess' voice rose several octaves. Liz finally intervened.

"Look, people are staring. Let's wrap up our food and get out of here." Liz followed through on her suggestion and the others mimicked her.

"We are staying at The Dairy, we could walk over there for a visit." Jack led the way. They were warmly greeted by Matt and Paul; who quickly settled them in the library and then closed the door for greater privacy. The cozy room had large walnut bookcases, an antique writing desk and two sets of dark green couches that faced each other over a coffee table. The wrappers were spread out and the group quickly finished their meal.

"Let's get this story straight, I was not shot. The bullet grazed my arm and I bled like a bucket of chum. We had an unexpected visitor on the ship. Missy wrestled a gun away from him after he fired a wild shot that accidentally grazed, and I do mean grazed, my arm. The doc on the ship stitched me up and I'm almost healed and ready for action. Now ladies where are we going to get the Blood? Do we have to bungy jump, take a speed boat or climb The Remarkables?"

Tess seemed to be barely keeping her emotions in check when she spoke. "Missy I want to thank you for helping Jack find me and for watching after him; I know he's a handful. If you and Liz would please excuse us for a bit, we need to speak privately."

Liz promptly jumped up. "Sure no problem; Missy and I can go and bug Matt and Paul for a few homemade goodies, bye." Liz grabbed Missy and pulled her from the room. As the door closed they could hear Missy's complaints until a silence confirmed that she had found the apricot turnovers.

Jack held up his good hand in mock supplication. "Honest, I am fine, don't start yelling . . ." He stopped as Tess gingerly slipped her arms around his neck. Her whispered endearments sent delicious shivers down his spine, straight to his groin. " So you missed me." He laughingly inquired.

"Yes, I missed you; however, my wild and wonderful nut-job, you are not going anywhere. You are going to stay put, under guard, at Wollstonecraft House while Deb and I retrieve the Flame. I don't care how resourceful you are, you are not trained for this mission and I won't endanger your life again."

"Wait, you need my help. I can take care of myself, even with the blasted cast!" Jack jumped up to emphasize his fitness. "If you don't let me go with you I'm going to tell President Thomson about the Tears."

"Jack, you are so darn cute; trying to blackmail me. You know, after all of this is over, I might make an honest man out of you. You certainly are good breeding material; intelligent, handsome, athletic and cunning." Tess was smiling as she looked him up and down.

"I mean it; I'm not bluffing."

"Well, the threat would hold more weight if I knew what the hell you were talking about." Tess began tapping a text on her phone.

"The Blood had fourteen smaller companion rubies called the Tears. They each represented the fourteen children of Mumtaz Mahal and Shan Jahan; those were taken by Sara along with the Blood and dozens of other priceless pieces in the leather bag. Besides yourself and a couple of others, I assume no one else knows. I grabbed the only piece of paper that mentions the Tears when I was in Mumbai; so if you want me to keep your golden hoard a secret, you had better deal me in." Jack crossed his arms in defiance. Tess half expected him to stomp his foot.

"Oh, Jack, you are 'tots adorbs,' as my students would say. Fine, you're right. We have always referred to the companion rubies as the Sparks, I suppose in reference to the Flame, however, you aren't going to say a word about anything to anyone, including Missy, from now on. You love me and you're not going to do anything to endanger my mission. I am a bit crazy about you and I'm not going to miss out on the first healthy relationship I have ever had with a man. We are taking you back to the house and you will stay put until Deb and I are finished; then you can give that cursed jewel back to the Indian people and we can spend Christmas back in Wyoming figuring out our future." Tess paused for breath.

"Wait, go back; did you just propose? Cause if you did, I'm in! I can't promise to not worry about you, but if you have enough protection then I won't stop you." Jack attempted to swoop Tess into his arms, however his romantic gesture failed because of his cast.

Tess laughingly untangled herself from his boyish embrace. "Alright, settle down. I wouldn't call that a proposal, I believe we have come to an understanding; let's just see where that takes us."

"Now suppose, and this is purely hypothetical, that I gave you my grandmother's diamond engagement ring for Christmas, would you graciously accept it and continue to think about marrying me or would you throw it back in my face?" Jack slipped his arms around her waist.

"Well, Jack, you're just going to have to 'cowboy up' and find out. Now, let's get you and Missy back to the house. Just pack an overnight bag, you won't need much." Tess watched as Jack happily sprang from the room, grabbed Missy and went down the hall.

"He looks pretty happy; what did you two do in there?" Liz raised her eyebrows in a comically melodramatic way.

"Jeez, nothing; you think I'm going to jump his bones in the library while all of you guys are enjoying High Tea in the parlor. I might have intimated that I would consider a proposal, that's all. Now can we leave all the love stuff aside for a minute. Theo and Alex want us back at the house, something is up." Tess thanked Matt and Paul, explained that their guests would return within forty-eight hours and walked out the front door; she was soon joined by Missy, Jack and Liz.

As they made their way on foot, Tess admired Queenstown. The single-story wood buildings, cobblestone arcade walks and street lamps reminded her of a typical American ski town. The entire village was festooned with colorful holiday lights and decorations. The odd juxtaposition of the ski/holiday theme against a blazing summer day made the entire experience surreal. She would never get used to

Christmas in the Southern hemisphere. The snowy mountains and plains of Wyoming were calling her home.

Now for her to-do list: find out what Theo and Alex were concerned about, contain Jack and Missy, do a final prep dive with Deb, keep the location of the Flame a secret, somehow get the ruby to the Indian embassy and (for her day job) post all of her student's final grades online. She could feel a wicked migraine coming on.

She watched as Liz walked warily next to Missy and Jack, who were involved in some sort of I Spy game. Those two were going to be a problem. She didn't believe Jack's assurances for a minute and Missy seemed equally unpredictable. They were going to have to call in the "big guns," to watch them; only Crystal could be trusted, Weston was just too darn nice.

They rounded the tree-lined drive and approached the house as Theo and Alex came scurrying out of the front door, falling over each other like lab puppies.

"Get inside quickly." An obviously flustered Alex grabbed Tess by her arm and began to drag her through the front door.

"Liz please get inside, something is up." Theo slipped his arm around her waist.

"Theo stop manhandling me, I already told you it's not going to happen." Liz laughingly pulled away and entered the house.

"Hey, a guy can try, you're only five years older than me, that's nothing. I like a woman with some experience." Theo continued his banter with Liz as they made their way down into the computer center.

Upon their arrival a few weeks ago, the brothers had descended on the Apple store. Now the room held at least a dozen black and steel workstations equipped with state-of-the-art computers. The walls were painted a light blue with white molding and they were covered in various screens, maps and blank white boards. Everyone's eyes were drawn to the massive screen hanging against the wall in the center of the room. It held a map of the world with blinking lights that looked like the heavens.

"Holy mother of God!" Missy stood in awe of the sheer size of the room.

"Jeez, the Sisterhood doesn't kid around when it comes to tech equipment. This looks like something out of James Bond." Jack looked at Tess.

"Yeah thanks, we were going for that look, wait never mind that! See what I mean!" Alex anxiously pointed to the screen.

"Um, nope." Liz echoed everyone's bewilderment.

"Alex, let's remember these guys are civilians." Theo stepped in front of the screen, picked up a tablet from a nearby desk and began to explain. "Everyone of the lights . . ." he used a curser to circle the various countries "represents one of our routing stations. If an unknown entity is trying to breach our security the light blinks. As you can see, we are experiencing an Armageddon scenario."

Leigh-Anne and Weston rushed into the room with Crystal on their heels. Crystal was the first to speak. "Shut it down, now! We can't take the chance that someone will break through!"

Theo held up his hands. "Alright; we will go dark, everyone just calm the frick down. Alex and I are going to contact all of our agents in the field, tell them to switch to the Number Stations and then we will shut down the system." The brothers dropped into chairs at their consoles and began furiously typing.

The rest of the group watched in dread as more and more lights began to flicker. Leigh-Anne stepped toward Alex.

"Alex shut it down now! If even one of those sites becomes compromised it could begin a chain reaction from which we will never recover. I mean it!"

"Wait, just, one, more, second." Sweat began to trickle down Alex's face as he and Theo frantically pounded away on their keyboards. Suddenly a loud clanging alarm reverberated through the room.

"Alex, Theo, now! Go dark or I will hit the override!" Leigh-Anne walked toward a panel on the wall as the huge screen went black and silence enshrouded the room.

"What in the Sam Hill just happened?" Missy looked back and forth between the brothers.

Theo was the first to speak. "We just experienced a catastrophic breach in our security system. We managed to shut it down right as the fail-safe default kicked in. As of now we are flying blind. I hope that we can reconfigure our systems to go back online, but right now we don't have any eyes or ears to the outside world."

"But who would have the international capability to crash a system as advanced as this?" Jack looked at Alex.

"Pretty much only one country; the U.S.. Ladies and gentleman I believe that we have just been hacked by our own government; I don't know why. As of right now, when Tess and Deb go for the dive we won't be able to monitor them from here. They will effectively be on their own." Alex, along with the rest of the group turned to look into the bewildered eyes of Tess.

CHAPTER TWENTY-ONE

"They're blind. Queenstown is eighteen hours ahead of us, so it would be mid afternoon there. I imagine that those folks will be spending the rest of today and tomorrow trying to get back online." A petit curvaceous red-headed tech turned her bright blue eyes toward President Thomson, her husband Rob, Nancy and Dave.

"Courtney, that's incredible; how on earth did you do it?" President Thomson leaned over the woman and peered at her console.

"This is pretty complicated Deep Web stuff. I can tell you that I began by using 1902 the year that Elizabeth Cady Stanton died and then I used 1906 the year that Susan B. Anthony died. I did include February 14, 1920, which is the date that Carrie Chapman Catt founded the non-partisan League of Women Voters at the last meeting of NAWSA. Other than that, it's the tricks of the trade. Do you need me to do anything else?" Courtney stood up and all but bowed to the president.

"No, thank you my dear; that was quite sufficient." The president shook hands with Courtney as she was shown out of the Oval Office by a Secret Service agent.

"Let's go to the residence." Rob unfolded his lanky six-foot two frame from a chair and led the three of them upstairs. As they settled into the expansive living room Nancy remembered that her friend had told her that presidents generally never used the Oval Office except for meetings or photo ops. President Thomson, like her predecessors, preferred to work in the private residence study.

"I took the liberty of ordering our favorite college food, Cubano sandwiches, from the kitchen. Since I am the only person 'with no dog in this hunt,' as it were, I need to remind you that what just happened was either illegal or as close as you can get to it." Rob's hazel eyes, a rich contrast to his jet-black hair, rested on Dave. Rob was more than qualified to make such a judgment; he had double majored in Law, Societies and Justice and Sociology with a minor in Political Science.

Dave walked over to the fireplace and began to methodically stack twisted sheets of paper, kindling and logs as he spoke. "We know. When you two approached us with the information regarding Jack and what he had stumbled upon, I was against inserting him into Nathan's group. Now we have temporarily shut down the Sisterhood. Hang the legality of it; what about Tess' protection during the retrieval. You say that your intel has provided you with the location of the Flame. Why don't you just send Navy Seals to get it?"

President Thomson joined Dave at the fireplace as he touched the pile with a match; flames jumped up as if they were electrified. "Dave we know you and Nancy are worried about Jack, so are we. I have the best men and women in the world working to protect him. From what we overheard, Jack won't even be on the boat. They are keeping he and Missy out of harms way at Wollstonecraft House. To answer your question, our divers would run out of air before they could find the right cave."

Dave looked around at the room's stately proportions. The carpet was a plush cream and it was dotted with richly colored silk rugs. The various couches and arm chairs ranged from soft muted pastels to vibrant floral. The coffee table and end tables were a gleaming oak.

The cream colored walls were covered in family photos. Even in this most hallowed building their friends had managed to make a comfy home. Dave loved and trusted them; he would have to believe that they knew best.

Nancy joined them as they contemplated the fire while Rob answered the gentle knock on the door. They were all silent as the waiters set up the late night dinner on the dining room table adjacent to the living room. When the food was arranged they solemnly sat down; each lost in their own worrying thoughts.

Nancy broke the morose silence. "Look, we are all playing a very dangerous game here and Jack's life might be in danger. We decided to crash their system so that no other country could breach it. That assumption may be incorrect. Hopefully, all of the focus is on Jack and Tess and not the Sisterhood. If we are very lucky, perhaps we can keep any interested parties from ever knowing the Sisterhood exists."

"Nancy's right." Rob agreed. "From everything that we can discern it looks as if the Russians and the Indians know about Tess and Jack. We don't have any other intelligence agencies popping up on our radar. The British are the ones that I worry about; MI5 and MI6 are particularly efficient. Those folks practically invented spy craft and their reach is longer than any other country's."

"I trust Jack; he is a very resourceful man. Just look at what he has already done." Dave counted off on his fingers. "He found the information on the Flame, then he infiltrated Nathan's group, he managed to grab Tess and even save her from a bear. Our son has been sadly underestimated. I would bet my life that he will somehow manage to follow Tess when she goes on the dive."

President Thomson looked startled. "He wouldn't! That could ruin the plans that we have set up so carefully. Although, now that you mention it, Jack has been pretty relentless in his pursuit of Tess."

"God, I could just wring his neck!" Nancy looked around the table at her friends.

"Nan, it's all going to work out; that's what I'm trying to say . . ."

"You don't know, you can't be sure . . ."

"I know, I am sure."

"You were always a hopeless optimist, my love." Nancy and Dave continued their back and forth as their friends watched in amusement. They had all been together a long time.

"Alright, let's assume Jack's going to do something incredibly foolhardy. Can we split the team and have half on Jack at the house and half on Hidden Island?" Nancy looked at President Thomson.

"No, sorry. We will keep Seal Team 6 on Hidden Island, but . . ." She raised her hand as Nancy began to object. " I will tell them to keep on the lookout for anyone, especially Jack, approaching the boat . Will that suffice?"

"Okay, that will have to do. I guess now that we have finished . . ." Nancy looked around the table at the empty plates, "we should call in the crew to set up."

President Thomson pushed a button near the light switch and there was an immediate knock. They watched as dishes were cleared by one crew, then another group came into the living room and managed, within an hour, to turn the place into a command center. The White House had a high-tech strategy room; this would be more private.

Courtney and another man stayed behind to run the system and explain it to the four friends. The man began.

"Okay, as of right now the mission is up and running. Seal Team 6 is in Queenstown and when night falls they will take two Zodiacs, that's a boat in case you are not familiar with the term . . ." He paused to look at the four of them as if they were decrepit relics from the Paleolithic era, "so the Zodiacs' engines have been adjusted to be as quiet as possible. The team will set up their sat com . . ." he paused again to make sure the old codgers were following, they nodded, bemused, "and then we have eyes and ears."

"Thank you Lance for that elucidating, if somewhat insulting, explanation. Now Courtney, I assume that the two of you will stay with us for the duration. Do either of you want anything?" President Thomson looked from one to the other as they shook their heads. "We will retire to the study, feel free to check in with us when the need arises."

Courtney made as if to raise her hand and then thought better of it. "Madam President, I do have one concern. I've been picking up some odd chatter for the last hour and I don't recognize the language. Let me pump up the volume." She turned her laptop toward the group and hit a key. A rapid-fire discussion was occurring.

"That's Portuguese; to be more precise, that is Brazilian Portuguese." Rob spoke five languages.

"Oh hell!" Nancy looked at the assembled group. "Courtney, where is the discussion taking place?"

"Well ma'am, let me try to find the specific location." Her fingers flew over the keys as she mumbled. "Dunedin, no four hours, Invercargill, nope that's two, Wanaka, shoot that's an hour away, Frankton, that could be, it's only fifteen minutes, wait, got it! There's a group of four speakers and they are in Queenstown on Park Street." Courtney looked up in triumph.

A sudden intake of breath caused Lance and Courtney to look from one to the other as the four friends collectively paled. Park Street ran along the beach that looked directly across Lake Wakatipu toward Hidden Island.

CHAPTER TWENTY-TWO

"Listen 'Short Attention Span Theater,' I'm trying to explain that his name was Lane Frost and our town is called Lane." Missy was attempting to finish her story.

"Hey, no need for name calling, I was just asking a question. You have to admit that his name being Lane and your town called Lane are confusing." Theo seemed to have switched his allegiance from Liz to Missy.

"So to continue my story, Lane Frost got the gold buckle as the world champion bull rider in 1987; then at the Cheyenne Frontier Days Rodeo in Wyoming on July 30, 1989, a bull hit him after he had dismounted. He had a bunch of broken ribs and when he tried to get away he fell and punctured his heart and lungs; he was only twenty-five when he died that day." Missy looked down as Theo watched.

"Yeah, it's a real sad story. He went to my old school Atoka High. His parents Elsie and Clyde have given away over three hundred thousand Bibles in his memory. They made a movie about his life called 8 Seconds; it was released in

1994." Missy looked up as Deb and Tess entered the living room. Jack sprung to life from inside a navy blue overstuffed chair by the window.

"So how was the hike?" Jack enquired of the women. For peace of mind, Tess had told Jack that she and Deb would be hiking to a secret cave to retrieve the Flame. She was only telling half a lie.

Deb dropped down on the light colored, hardwood floor and began a series of stretches. "It was great. The Remarkables are stunning and we even saw a couple of patches of snow. But we are wringing wet. I'm going to shower then we will need to carbo load for dinner if tomorrow's hike is going to be longer." She jumped up and went down the hall toward her room.

Jack walked over to Tess and gathered her in his arms. "Gross, you don't want my sweat on you, let me go and shower." Tess attempted to squirm free.

"Not so fast my little chickadee." Jack began to nibble on her neck and whisper in her ear.

"Hey, do you mind! The rest of us are getting ready to have dinner, yeesh." Theo looked longingly at Missy as Jack continued unabated.

Tess managed to wrangle free from his very insistent attentions. "I'm going to hit the shower and then I'll meet you out on the veranda for dinner." She walked down the hall and turned left into the bedroom that she and Jack now shared.

"So, Theo, what's going on with IT?" Jack walked with Missy and Theo as they headed into the kitchen to join Alex, who was putting the finishing touches on dinner. He was making a traditional Greek Pastichio, a type of lasagna from his grandmother's recipe. The entire household had become addicted to Greek food after the boys had arrived. Using their Yiayia's, as Greek grandmother's were called, special ingredients, they turned even the most ordinary dishes into masterpieces.

Theo joined Alex at the massive range. "We have located all of our agents and told them to stand down for the duration of the mission here. We will maintain radio silence until the Flame has been retrieved and returned to the Indian government."

Alex continued. "So basically, we have shut everything down in hopes that once the heat is off we can go back to business. Our systems were not breached so we should be good to go. Theo and I have taken the downtime to make sure that the encryption keys are heavily complex in the firewall's programming; they should withstand any future assault."

As Alex and Theo concentrated on finishing up the homemade bread and Greek salad, the group was joined by Nana and Papa.

"Chester, Ruth, could I interest you in a glass of wine? We have a fabulous red from Healdsburg, California." Jack began to open a bottle of wine.

"Honey, we told you to call us Nana and Papa, everyone does. Until you arrived I don't think anyone knew our real names." Nana's impish face crinkled up in a smile. Nana and Papa looked like twins. They were both mid-five feet in stature, grey haired and wiry of body. The where in excellent shape for their age. The fact that they bicycled, hiked, swam or walked everyday attested to their general good health.

"Ruthie's right son, we hardly ever use our God-given names. This way it makes us feel as if we are grandparents to all of you." Papa patted Jack on the back. Like most people, he had taken an immediate liking to Jack.

Jack settled his future grandparents-in-law at the long farm table on the veranda overlooking the lake. What a wonderful family he would (hopefully) be marrying into. He had been heartbroken the night that Tess had told him her life story. Losing one's parents and being savagely beaten and almost raped at such a young age had left more than physical scars on the woman he loved.

As he poured wine in Nana's, Papa's, Missy's and his glasses; he pondered his future. He looked around the table as Weston, Leigh-Anne, Liz, Crystal, Deb and Tess joined the company. When Alex and Theo brought the food and sat down the little family was complete. So this was it. These were the people that Jack would spend the rest of his life with. He had no illusions about Missy. She would never go back to her old life after this. She might still teach in Australia, but she would spend her break doing the same work as Tess.

Missy would need to be trained, but he knew eventually she would join the Flame Throwers. He looked longingly at Tess as she favored him with a radiant smile. He didn't have a choice. From the moment he had sat in on her first lecture, skulking in the dark in the back of the large auditorium, he had been captivated. Now he would have to watch her walk out the door every summer and never know if she would return.

It would be a very tenuous life, however, he could never walk away now; his decision was irrevocable. "I propose a toast. In two day's time Tess and Deb will hike to who knows where and retrieve the Blood from a hidden cave. I want to wish them Godspeed with a traditional Celtic blessing my grandmother used to pray over us.

May the road rise up to meet you.

May the wind be always at your back.

May the sun shine warm upon your face.

May the rain fall soft upon your fields,

and until we meet again,

May God hold you in the palm of his hand.

Everyone raised their glasses as streams of tears silently fell down Nana's face. Tess jumped up and gathered her grandmother in her arms. "Man, Jack, look, you made my Nana cry. Let's cheer up this crowd." Tess sat down between her grandparents as Alex and Theo spontaneously burst into song. Missy (who was the only person startled by this display) had obviously never been to Greece or spent anytime around Greeks.

The singing, drinking (except Deb and Tess) and eating (including the most delicious baklava anyone had ever had) continued until ten o'clock when everyone went off to their various rooms. As Jack and Tess snuggled into the middle of their king-sized bed they looked out through the sliding glass doors at the lake.

"So one more day of training and then the retrieval hike. Are you sure you're feeling okay? You seem extra tired." Jack began to rub the monumental knots out of Tess' shoulders.

"Yep, don't worry about me, I'm tough as beef jerky. We will be very methodical with our practice tomorrow. Every movement will be slow and steady. I am looking forward to getting the Flame and returning to Wyoming in time for Christmas. It seems as if this mission will never end." Tess sighed and closed her eyes.

"Right, because your life is so normal at any given time." Jack chuckled.

"Hey, I lead a normal life! I work on the ranch, teach at the university, drink locally brewed beers at the Bucket of Blood Saloon in town on the weekends. Other than the summers when I am a bit more busy, my life is absolutely normal." Tess smiled at the absurdity of her statement.

"Sure, absolutely normal, except for the, 'putting your life on the line,' part of the summer."

"Jack, you can't ask me to give that up. I won't do it. You take Flame Thrower and all or nothing." Tess turned to look into his eyes.

"I know, I will, I do. If Sara and your Nana could make it work, then you and I can. Please just tell me that you want kids. That would be a deal breaker." Jack frowned and looked down.

"Oh, Jack, of course I want kids. We have plenty of room for half a dozen little guys and gals. Elizabeth Cady Stanton had seven. That might be a bit much, but we could shoot for three or four." Tess wrapped her arms around her future husband.

She hated lying to him about the dive tomorrow, but it was the right thing to do. She and Deb would get the dive over, the Flame would be returned and Jack would be mollified by their Christmas in Wyoming. Tess had become more homesick as she read all of her office emails from the university. The little items such as Dr. Kim's retirement party, the professors' Christmas caroling through town and the Boy Scouts' tree sale, resonated much more deeply this year.

"Hello, hello, whatcha thinking about?" Jack began his usual amorous advances. He was pretty adorable; Tess decided to keep him. She enthusiastically threw herself into their very boisterous love making until Jack finally passed out around midnight.

The iridescent minutes flashed by on the bedside clock until four, when Tess slowly moved from Jack's slack arms. She dressed quickly and quietly, then, like a sleek shadow, she slipped out the door. Deb, Weston, Leigh-Anne, Liz and Crystal were waiting in the living room.

Leigh-Anne went into CEO mode. "Alright, let's get this party started. Weston and Liz will be topside while Deb and Tess do the dive. Any more people abroad might draw unwanted attention. You guys are just out on a fishing trip, that's all, remember to keep the scuba gear covered. Crystal and I will stay here and act as if Deb and Tess are off on their usual hike. Missy and Jack have bought the story so far; I don't think they will question it for one more day."

"The lake is perfect today, nice and quiet and at a low point. I don't anticipate any problems for my little sis and her Dutch goddess of a friend." Weston smiled and the entire group relaxed. He had an inner core of self-assuredness that was contagious.

"Thanks Weston; I'm going to mention that description to my husband when I get home. I am pumped! I've been blasting Adele songs through my ear buds and I am ready to go." Deb threw her arm around Tess' shoulder.

"I'm ready; let's do this." Tess was feeling a bit queasy as she went into the kitchen to toast a couple of pieces of the bread leftover from last night. She was soon joined by Nana and Papa who looked worried enough for the entire group. Deb ate just as sparingly as Tess. They needed a bit on their stomachs but not enough to bother them while diving. They could make up for it when they surfaced.

Crystal came into the kitchen as Tess and Deb fiercely hugged Nana and Papa good-bye. "Ladies let's go." She ushered the two women out to the truck where Weston and Liz waited with the diving gear. Weston and Leigh-Anne loaded up the gear as Liz climbed in, followed by Weston.

Crystal grabbed both Deb and Tess by the arms as they turned toward the truck. "Deb, Tess, I have a very bad feeling about this. Promise me that you will be ever vigilant on this dive. No mistakes. Just get in the damn water, retrieve that cursed jewel and get the hell out of there. At the first sign of trouble abort the mission; do you understand?" Deb and Tess solemnly bobbed their heads in unison.

Little did they know.

CHAPTER TWENTY-THREE

"I'm sorry Papa, it's really bad manners to beat you like a dog. My Mama and Daddy taught me better than that." Missy raked in dozens of poker chips as Crystal, Jack and Papa laughed.

"Don't worry your pretty little poker genius head about it darlin'. I'll just get more from Jack the next time around. Son, are you sure you're from Montana? You are the worst poker player I've ever met." Papa slapped Jack on the back as Leigh-Anne and Nana laughed from the other table on the veranda.

"Well, we couldn't have chosen a more beautiful setting to pick Jack's pockets." Missy continued. "Jack and I stopped in Wellington for a day and I fell in love with the city. It reminded me of San Francisco, with the bay and all. The cutest thing I have ever seen was the penguin road crossing signs. I thought they were making it up for the tourists until we saw actual penguins come out of the water and cross one of the roads. I absolutely love New Zealand. It's not just the stunning scenery; the people here are some of the nicest folks I have ever met in my life."

Crystal and Leigh-Anne had tried to get Missy and Jack out of the house with numerous inducements, including a trip to Fergburger, to no avail. It was as if Jack knew something different was a foot. Crystal had noticed that Jack seemed almost prescient when it came to Tess. It was going to be a long morning.

Jack had been pacing back and forth on the veranda when Papa, bless his heart, had proposed a game of poker. Missy, for obvious reasons, had jumped at the idea as she led Jack to the table. Crystal had joined in to keep an eagle eye on Jack. He seemed restless and he kept looking at the time on his cell.

Crystal would be relieved when this mission was over. The chilling feeling of dread would not go away. She knew that Deb and Tess were in good hands with Liz and Weston. The equipment was in pristine condition and the two women were very experienced divers. It really wasn't the dive portion of the mission Crystal was worried about. There was no question that Weston and Liz would provide ample security.

Crystal found herself standing at the railing looking out over the mist shrouded lake wondering how the dive was going and if they were almost finished. She shook the feeling of foreboding from her and moved away from the railing. She didn't want Jack to see her looking apprehensively at the lake.

"Hey, please don't fault the great state of Montana for this native son. I've been told that I can't keep my face straight, I have a 'tell,' and I'm a horrible bluffer. Good thing I don't have to make a living from this. By the way, did I mention that I am gainfully employed again?" Jack looked around at the surprised faces.

"Yep, Dr. Kim, the medievalist at Tess' university just retired and I sent my resume in and did a video conference interview. They seemed a bit surprised that I wanted the job considering the rather isolated location of the campus, but I assured them that I was ready to settle down. I start in February after the winter break. I'm saving it as a surprise for Tess." Jack was beaming as Nana jumped up and hugged him.

"Oh, honey, that is great news. Now we can all go home together. I have missed Jameson, harsh winters and all." Nana gave Jack a kiss on the head and rejoined Leigh-Anne.

A soft breeze rippled the water of the lake as one by one each of them turned to view the beautiful sight. The warm sun shone down upon the veranda with its combination of wood ranch style table and white wicker chairs placed conveniently around the expanse.

The poker players sat in the chairs with a matching large round wicker table. Nana and Leigh-Anne were placed in chairs facing the water. All of the friends were wearing shorts and tee shirts in anticipation of the ever-warming summer day.

"Jack that is wonderful news. I'm happy that you finally decided to stay in one place and you somehow managed to find a woman crazy enough to put up with you." Missy gave Jack a teasing poke.

"Man, you are tough. First you get Papa to besmirch my dubious poker playing abilities and now you act as if you had to tie a jewel around my neck to get Tess to notice me. Wait, now that I think about it, that's kind of what happened." Jack was joined in his laughter by everyone on the veranda, as Theo and Alex arrived carrying trays laden with food.

"What is it with you two? Why are you always trying to feed us?" Missy was only joking; she happened to be their best customer.

"We're Greek." Theo and Alex answered in unison as everyone tucked into the various dishes they set on the table.

"Wait, so no matter what I ask you, if it seems self-evident, the answer is, 'We're Greek?'" Missy sat down at the table with a heaping plate of food.

Alex answered for his brother. "We're Greek; we love wine, women and song, not necessarily in that order. Food and family are in there too."

Theo sat down next to Missy and continued with his brother's line of thought. "Alex is right; family is everything to us. We have come to think of all of you as family now. Take Tess and Deb for instance. I'm looking out at that beautifully calm water and I'm relieved . . ." Theo stopped in mid sentence as he looked at Jack with a horrified expression. There was a collective intake of breath as everyone looked from Jack to Missy.

"Wait, what did you just say about the lake?" Jack jumped up and knocked over several plates of food. The smashing of the crockery broke the stunned silence.

"Nothing, I was just thinking about going for a swim and how refreshing it would be for Tess and Deb when they get back from their hike, that's all nothing else." Theo looked ashen as Jack closed on him.

"Don't lie to me. We spent months together and I know when you are lying. What the hell does the lake have to do with Tess and Deb today? Someone better tell me what is going on before I shake it out of Theo." Jack grabbed Theo by his shirt and pulled him off his feet.

"Hold up son, drop that boy right now." Papa stood up and released Theo from Jack's angry grasp. "I don't see any harm in telling you what's going on now. The girls have probably already finished with their dive and they should be heading back within the hour. Tess and Deb are diving to an underwater cave to retrieve the Flame; that's all, no big deal."

"Papa's right; Alex just got off the HAM with Liz and she said that Tess and Deb have given the, 'tug three times,' signal on the descent line to say that they have the Flame and they are heading up. It's a really deep dive so it will take them a bit, but they have plenty of oxygen and Weston and Liz don't anticipate any problems. Jack it's no big deal. Tess and Deb are experienced divers so you don't need to worry." Theo tried to pat Jack on the shoulder as Jack shook him off.

"No big deal!!! You don't know what you have done!!! It's not Deb and Tess I'm worried about!!! It's the baby!!! Any kind of dive could affect the baby, especially a deep dive!!!" Jack began to run around the side of the house toward the cars. Missy shook herself out of her stunned position and ran after Jack. The sound of a car hurriedly revving up galvanized the rest of the group as everyone ran around the corner of the house toward the garage.

Crystal grabbed Jack by the shoulders as Missy gunned the engine. "What baby?!!! What the hell are you talking about?!!! Deb would have told us if she were pregnant. She wouldn't have even agreed to do the dive if she had known her condition would make it dangerous for a baby. Jack, you are wrong. Deb is fine. You can't go running off like this. You will draw unwanted attention to the dive. For all anyone knows they are just off fishing."

"Deb's not having a baby, Tess is pregnant!!! She doesn't even know it!!! Sorry, Nana and Papa, but when Tess and I were together in Montana I poked tiny holes in the condoms to get her pregnant. When I arrived here I could tell by her listless behavior and her slight weigh gain that it worked." Jack was spun around by Papa, who proceeded to slam a fist the size of a ham into his face.

CHAPTER TWENTY-FOUR

"So Madame President, what should we do?" A man's voice enquired through the computer.

"Wait, just wait, you're telling us that you can see a Zodiac with three people aboard heading towards the boat?" President Thomson motioned to Courtney to join her by the computer. "Please use your telescopic lens to show us the occupants."

Rob, Nancy and Dave hovered around the computer as Courtney's fingers flew across the keys. A flickering image began to develop on the screen. "I'm trying to use the zoom but the boat is moving pretty fast. If you want us to intercept it we need to leave the island now. I can see two females: one tall with long blonde hair and one mighty formidable lookin' red head. The lone male's face and shirt are covered in blood and he has a cast on one arm. I don't see any weapons, I repeat, no weapons in evidence." The voice stopped as the boat came into view on the White House computer.

"Oh, my God! That's Jack and Missy! I don't know who the other woman is. What happened? Why is Jack bloody and what happened to his arm?" Nancy turned to Dave as President Thomson picked up the dropped conversation.

"Do not intercept; I repeat, do not intercept that Zodiac. They are friendlies. Please continue your update." President Thomson pulled a chair closer to the screen as they watched Jack and the two women arrive and board the boat. There was a good deal of wild hand gesturing among the five occupants until an understanding appeared to have been reached. All of the people on the boat sat down and seemed to lose themselves in a very serious conversation.

"Okay, as I was saying. We set up on Hidden Island at 0400 hours this morning. The night was quiet and warm; with just a bit of a low mist on the lake. The mist made it difficult for us to see the boat with the diving group until they were almost fifty yards out. They must have done something to modify the boat's engines because they were extremely quiet." The unidentified male paused for a moment and then continued.

"We observed two females put on wet suites and scuba gear, while the other two, one male one female, helped them. The women went into the water about twenty minutes ago. The male keeps checking the descent line and the female spends most of her time on the HAM radio. We couldn't believe that they were using an 'old school,' HAM radio system, considering the boat is state-of-the-art." He paused for the obvious recognition of this anomaly.

Dave was the only person to react. "So they are using the most basic mode of communication on board. They could have used Very High Frequency referred to as VHF which generally needs a line of sight and is used mostly boat to boat or Single Side Band called SSB, which has a longer range. With HAM they use repeaters placed around, especially on mountains. You guys must have heard of HAM radio operators. My dad used to be big into it after WWII." Everyone looked at Dave waiting for a bit more clarification.

He tried again. "Look the HAM system is best for lake to HQ communications because both VHF and SSB won't work around the curves and mountains. The Sisterhood seems to be very resourceful when it comes to guarding their private conversations."

"Right, now all three have gone digital, and it is more difficult to crack their various encryption systems, however, we finally intercepted their communications and it all seems to be going well. The divers should be up within the next few minutes." He paused.

"Well, since you are monitoring the boat's conversations, have they said anything about the new arrivals?" President Thomson enquired.

"Yes, ma'am. The woman is on the radio again saying something about Papa punching Jack and breaking his nose, Missy almost knocking down Crystal, Weston wants to speak to Leigh-Anne and Tess is pregnant. Does any of that make sense?" The man waited for a response. Everyone but Courtney began to speak at once.

"Hey man, congrats! You're going to be a grandpa! That's awesome!" Rob was hugging a clearly shocked Dave.

"Thanks Rob. I don't even know what to say. I'm happy; I know that." Dave said.

Nancy looked at her best friend. "What in the hell?"

"It appears that Jack somehow managed to get Tess pregnant. Nan, you and Dave are going to be grandparents." President Thomson stood up and hugged a frozen looking Nancy.

"Wait, when did that irresponsible son of mine have time to get Tess pregnant?!!!" Nancy looked bemused.

"According to what I am hearing, Jack messed with the contraceptive on purpose so that he could get Tess pregnant and trap her in some sort of reverse 1950's marriage plot. Tess does not know and Jack is worried that the dive could hurt the baby." The Seal Team 6 member was running a play-by-play commentary.

"Ma'am, if I might interject. If this woman Tess is in the first trimester the baby should be fine. I wouldn't recommend diving, but more than likely the baby will be okay." The man stopped as Courtney visibly jumped in her chair.

"Hang on a minute! Madame President I'm picking up that Portuguese chatter again. Could your husband translate?" Courtney placed her large black headphones over Rob's ears.

"Okay, they are confused. They were supposed to be meeting three, no wait, two people called Vladimir and Estragon. That can't be right, they are the main characters in the play Waiting for Godot. I guess those could be their code names; if so, this is an oddly literate group of thieves. That's kind of funny, because in the play, Godot never shows up, most people think that Godot is God, hang on. Now they have decided to leave. Their plane departs within the hour and they are heading to the airport." Rob handed the headphones back to Courtney.

She slipped them on for a few minutes and then pulled them from her head. "Yep, he's right. I just heard them hail a taxi and then lots of shuffling, then nothing. Hopefully, they are gone. Do you want me to do a language sweep of Queenstown to see if I can pick up anymore intel on the Vladimir and Estragon characters?"

"Thanks Courtney, if you would keep it up that would be great. I know it's the height of the tourist season in New Zealand, and there are bound to be hundreds of people in Queenstown speaking several different languages, but let's be vigilant." President Thomson motioned to her friends and they all sat down in front of the computer as Courtney moved to Lance's computer a few feet away.

"Madame President, do you want me to continue with my recon?" The male voice was back.

"Yes, please, sorry for the interruption; we are trying to do several things at once here."

"I hear that ma'am, I guess that happens every moment of everyday at the White House. So from what I gather you have the baby's grandparents with you. Please tell them that I have been a PADI certified diver since I was thirteen years old and the baby should be fine. That doesn't mean that the lady Tess should do any more dives. She needs to take it easy." He was interrupted by the bemused chuckles of four very concerned people.

The thought of Tess, "taking it easy," was beyond comprehension. Tess was in the middle of the dive of her life, with the fate of the Sisterhood hanging in the balance and she was pregnant. Nancy was alternatively excited about becoming a grandmother and worried about Jack and Tess. Gradually the realization of the situation dawned on her. Jack, and for that matter their entire family, would be irrevocably tied to Tess.

All plans for breaking the two of them up vanished. Nancy considered her position. She was relieved that Jack would live close by in Wyoming and she was excited about being a grandmother. Tess as a daughter-in-law was another matter. Nancy did have the power within the Sisterhood to limit Tess' exposure to dangerous assignments. However, would Tess accept being reined in; the answer would be, no.

"So everyone on the boat seems to have calmed down except the tall blonde; she is waving her arms around and yelling. The big fella is looking over the starboard side. I assume the two women are coming up. The woman on the HAM is telling her HQ that she will let them know the minute Tess and Deb surface. The bloody guy, I guess that's Jack, is having his nose packed by the fierce looking red head." He paused to take a breath.

"Great work. I want your team to scan every inch of that lake. When Tess and Deb surface I don't want any surprises. Let's confirm that your orders are to let the women get back on the boat and then you will intercept them on the lake. I don't want any of this happening at the dock. When you board their boat, hand your satellite phone to Jack and he will handle everything from there. Is that understood?" President Thomson said.

"Yes, ma'am, understood. We will intercept, identify ourselves and proceed aboard the minute they stow their diving gear and get underway. Don't worry, we are watching all areas around the boat. So far everything . . ." his voice trailed off as shouting could be heard in the background. "Madame President, we have a Zodiac coming fast on the port side of the boat with two armed men. Permission to intercept, repeat, permission to intercept!!!" The man yelled into the phone.

"Yes, go, go, go, for God sakes, don't let anything happen to the people on that boat or I will have your hide!!!" President Thomson and her friends watched helplessly as the video link of the boat abruptly ended with the sound of gunfire in the background.

CHAPTER TWENTY-FIVE

The diving conditions couldn't have been better. The lake was like glass with barely a ripple to mar the pristine surface. There was a nice low mist that had concealed their departure from the main marina in Queenstown. They had quietly motored out to within fifty yards of Hidden Island.

Weston and Liz had helped them with their five-millimeter wet suits, weight belts, oxygen tanks and masks while Tess and Deb checked their regulators to make sure the air was turned on and that nothing was blocking the mechanism. The regulator, backup regulator and air pressure gage, each had their own hose that were connected to the air tank through a fitting known as an octopus.

The air tank was filled with compressed air. Which consists of the regular air that we breath forced into the tank with a compressor. Outside air is twenty-one percent oxygen. If you were to breath pure oxygen it would make you light-headed. Liz double checked the oxygen flow and handed them their flippers.

Weston turned off the boat and hit the wench that lowered the anchor. Then Deb and Tess climbed down three stairs at the stern, sat down on the bright blue fiberglass swim platform, put on their fins, gave the thumbs up sign to Weston and silently slid into the water. The last sight in Tess' vision was a worried looking Liz making the sign of the cross over their heads.

Tess felt as if she were snuggling into the welcome embrace of an old friend; she dove the waters of Lake Wakatipu every chance she could get. When Nana had informed Tess, at her college graduation, that she was now in charge of the Flame's hiding place, Tess knew exactly where she would place it.

She had discovered the underwater cave system on a deep diving trip several years earlier. The lake did not offer the same spectacular fish, such as you would see at their famous neighbor, the Great Barrier reef, however, it held its own mystery. With one exception, Lake Wakatipu was a very safe diving spot.

So far, she and Deb had not seen tail nor teeth, of the only dangerous predator in the lake. Tess hoped that their luck would hold. At least they didn't have to worry about Great White sharks.

Before they had gotten into the water, Deb and Tess had inflated their Buoyancy Control Devices or BCD's. They confirmed with each other that they were ready to descend. Then they deflated their BCD's by hitting the release button and began their descent. This was where the weight belt came into play. Since the human body, air tanks and the wetsuit are buoyant the weight assures that the diver has negative buoyancy so that you can descend.

As they slowly moved down into the water they equalized the pressure in their ears by pinching their noses and blowing out every three to five feet. This was a tedious but essential practice that assured the pressure from the outside of your body would be equal with the inner ear pressure so that you didn't burst an eardrum.

They were both wearing dive computers on their wrists, which they carefully monitored to watch their rate of descent and depth. Some divers didn't even use the wrist computers, however, this was a particularly challenging dive and both women wanted to be prepared. The old computers were usually black on gray, but for the last twenty years, models were backlit so they were extremely easy to read.

Tess marveled at the silence of the mountain lake. The feeling of utter peace that came from being deep under water was the reason that she had taken up scuba diving. It seemed that nowhere on land could a person experience the quiet majesty of nature, and the serenity of soundlessness.

Tess motioned to Deb as she led her toward the underwater cave. Tess had placed the huge ruby in a metal water-tight case. Since it was a freshwater lake there was no worry about the corrosive effects of saltwater. The mid morning light filtered through the crystalline water casting shadows across the slowly undulating lake grasses. Deb and Tess turned on their flashlights as they made their way into the cave.

Deb anxiously checked her wrist as Tess sent her a reassuring thumbs up. They still had plenty of oxygen in their tanks. Tess led the way deeper into the cave as the light slowly faded, leaving the flashlights as their sole source of navigation. Just two more turns to the left and they were there. Tess moved an outsized boulder, ran her hand under a ledge and pulled on a handle.

Deb's eyes lit up as she spied the black box that held the world's largest ruby. Tess understood the allure of the stone; everyone loved a treasure hunt. Deb detached a dark green webbed sack from her leg and handed it to Tess. Tess slipped the sack over the box and checked her dive computer. Time to go. They had used up fifteen minutes of air in the cave.

Tess and Deb each grabbed a section of the sack and slowly made their way forward with Tess slightly in front. As they came out of the mouth of the cave Tess saw a massive black body slithering through the lake grass. Oh, hell!!! Hopefully Deb hadn't seen it. She looked worriedly over her shoulder at her friend but Deb was looking back at the mouth of the cave. Good.

They stopped swimming as they reached the dive line and gave it the agreed upon three tugs. Slowly they begin their ascent by slightly inflating their BCD's. They had to adjust for the weight of the box and they made sure to breath evenly.

Their lungs were automatically adjusting to the lack of pressure as they ascended by expanding. It was critical at this juncture that they breathe normally because if you held your breath your lungs could explode. They rose side by side with one hand across their chests and one hand holding the sack. They slowly swished their fins in unison as they made sure to not rise faster than their air bubbles.

Everything was going according to plan as they checked their dive computers and halted at the fifteen-foot safety stop. They had to wait three minutes to help release some of the trapped gases, such as nitrogen, in their bodies. Tess peered anxiously around to look for any unwanted guests. She spied at least a dozen black bodies slowly congregating beneath them.

Unfortunately, Deb's eyes followed Tess'. A scream bubbled from Deb as she attempted to ascend. Tess grabbed her shoulders and held her down as she counted the minutes until they could escape.

Deb locked eyes with Tess as the eels raced up and enveloped them in a swirling mass of writhing black. Deb knew. She had seen these predators on the Animal Planet show River Monsters. That was the memory she could not retrieve when Leigh-Anne and Liz had mentioned the lake.

Jeremy Wade, the host of the show, had talked about these massively muscular carnivorous Longfin eels, which could weigh over fifty pounds and grow to over six feet in length. They were not electric but their blood was toxic; even a small amount could kill a human.

Deb was frozen in terror as she watched Tess counting down the seconds. The Longfin's were known to attack in packs. They would go into a frenzy and bite flesh with their hundreds of reverse facing pointy teeth; then they went into a "death roll," just like a crocodile.

Tess held onto Deb's shoulders gently squeezing them to reassure her as the seconds dragged on. Tess' point of view was not so dire. Sure the eels were carnivorous, however, she had come across them many times and they hadn't attacked. Granted she had never been in the midst of this many in a pack, but she assumed that even if they nipped at them a bit, they would make it back to the boat.

Five-millimeter wet suits were pretty tough. Tess could see where even with the thick wet suit those hundreds of sharp teeth could tear through. Her greatest concern was if they broke the skin and caught the scent of blood, they would react like sharks. So far, they seemed more curious than agitated. The trick was to move as languidly as the eels floating around them.

While the Longfins continued to circle them a couple became more bold as they rubbed up against the women and their tanks. Tess tried to keep in mind that for centuries the Maori had treasured the Longfin as a food source (when cooked, they were not toxic) and a good luck charm. They even had a legend about a monster Longfin called Taniwha.

Deb wasn't so sanguine. She was shaking uncontrollably as the eels continued their inspection. Tess looked at her computer and gave the final ascent signal. Those three short minutes felt like a lifetime. As they rose together with the ruby between them the movement seemed to set off some sort of signal.

The eels began to bump into them. Almost gently at first, then with a more aggressive approach. One huge monster, easily over five feet, slammed into Tess' mask. She struggled to right her equipment as her oxygen tank took a direct hit. Deb was bearing the full weight of the ruby as she attempted to pull out her diving knife.

Tess grabbed her section of the sack with one hand and fixed her mask with the other. A quick check on her wrist assured her that she had plenty of air. Suddenly an eel swept around Deb and somehow managed to grab hold of her octopus and yank the breathing tube. Deb's oxygen line was severed.

Deb tried to remain calm. She knew that they were just a couple of feet from the surface of the lake. She could hold her breath for even longer than she would need. As she tried to free her diving knife a regulator came into view.

Tess was "buddy breathing," or sharing her oxygen. Deb smiled and took a couple of deep breaths before handing the regulator back. Tess signaled to not use the dive knife. Deb realized what she was doing. She remembered that the Longfin were like sharks. If she stabbed one, the blood from that would send the rest into a frenzy and they might never make it to the boat.

Deb decided to stay calm and not make any sudden movements that might appear aggressive. At almost that precise moment she felt a tug on her left fin. Hell, those monsters were pulling her. She looked on in horror as one of the giant eels bit into Tess' leg. Mercifully, not a drop of blood floated out. The eel must not have broken the skin.

With one last breath from their shared regulator they broke the water's surface, lunged for the bobbing blue swim platform and hurled themselves a top it as the eels swarmed in a mass beneath them. Deb screamed in agony as an eel latched on to her ankle. Blood spurted everywhere.

Tess bludgeoned the eel with the metal box and kicked its inert body into the water. The lake beneath them was roiling with blood and black snake-like bodies as the women stumbled up the stairs and collapsed onto the boat.

"My, my, those are nasty little buggers aren't they. Good thing you made it back in almost one piece. Now if you will just hand over the Flame, I won't have to shoot you." A grinning man leveled a gun at Deb and Tess as they struggled to their knees.

CHAPTER TWENTY-SIX

"Screw you." Tess lunged toward the port side of the boat, stood up and dangled the black box over the edge. "I'll drop it in and you can feed the damn fish with your stinking flesh."

Crystal, arms raised, moved between Tess and the man. "Hold on. Let's all calm down. Tess, this gentleman. . .", she pointed to the tall man with curly blonde hair, "is Vladimir and his friend . . .", she waved her hand toward a short dark haired man holding a gun on Weston, "is Estragon. They would like to trade our lives for the Flame. Let's just hand it over and be done with this."

Tess looked from one gunman to the other. "Wait, you two losers used code names from Waiting for Godot? That's the lamest . . ." Tess was interrupted by Estragon.

"Vlad, we got company." He turned and fired toward an approaching Zodiac then brought his gun around and trained it back on Weston. No shots were returned.

"Right, so you are the tough one. So be it. I noticed that you have been shooting glances at the gimp over there." He stopped and pointed his gun at Jack sitting next to Liz on starboard side benches.

"Hey, I'm perfectly capable of defending myself." Jack attempted to stand up but Liz put a restraining hand on his shoulder as he eased back down.

"So I'm guessing he means something to you. How about I shoot him and see if that changes your mind." He leveled his gun at Jack's right knee.

"Stop, stop, right now." Crystal tried to draw Vladimir's attention. "Look we will hand it over and you can go. Obviously someone in the boat you just shot up is after the Flame as well. You can take your chances in the water against them. My friend is bleeding profusely, please let us tend to her and we will give you the jewel. No one needs to get hurt."

"Fine." Vladimir agreed as Missy grabbed the first aid kit and knelt down beside a writhing Deb. She expertly tended to the cleaning and dressing of the wound while the rest of the group looked on. The entire bottom of the boat was awash with saltwater and blood.

"There, see, we can be reasonable. Now give me the case and we will be on our way. Of course, we will need a little insurance. What do you say Estragon, should we take the blonde nurse, the big redhead or that gorgeous Latina? We can't bring the hellcat with the box. She looks like first chance she gets she would kill us, cook us and then eat us." Vladimir looked at his partner.

Estragon sneered a reply. "You know me, I like me some blondes. Since the other one is lame we might as well take Nurse Nancy."

"Okay, far be it from me to take away the simple pleasures in life. Get up Blondie." Vladimir pointed his gun at Missy and made a rising motion. Missy raised her hands in the air and stood up.

"No." Tess shoved Crystal out of the way and locked eyes with Vladimir. "No one is leaving this boat. I'll tell you what Vladdie my boy, you are dead and you don't even know it. I am going to kill you and your partner and I'm going to skin you and wear you like a coat."

As Estragon and Vladimir began to laugh the final set pieces were moved into place. The two men didn't seem to know or care that they were on a boat with a unit. Weston, Crystal, Liz and Tess were as effective as a machine gun. All of their combined years of training came to the fore.

Without even speaking or formulating a plan, the four of them instinctively locked into synchronicity. Tess had purposely shoved Crystal toward Missy and Deb. Then Crystal had immediately taken a protective stance in front of the two women.

Liz had managed to slide down the bench near the bow where the flare gun was kept. While all eyes were riveted on Vladimir and Tess, Liz was inching her way toward the gun holster.

Meanwhile, Weston had imperceptibly moved closer to Estragon. Liz just needed a few more seconds and they would all be ready. Tess had to stall for time. Jack had somehow figured out the situation. He jumped up to block Vladimir's view of Liz.

"Honey, honey, let's have no more talk of killing, skinning and the wearing of people coats. If Nana and Papa could hear you now." Jack blithely walked toward Tess, thus drawing all eyes away from the bow of the boat. He slipped his good arm around her shoulders. "Honestly, you even scare me sometimes. Well Vlad, women, what can you do with them?" Jack forced a little man-to-man chuckle, then all hell broke loose.

A megaphone from the other boat squeaked and came to life. "You two men on the boat, drop your weapons, I repeat, drop your weapons. We have you in our sights and we will shoot to kill." It was just the distraction they needed. Liz sprung to life as if she had been hit by lightning.

Liz lunged for the flare gun as Vladimir trained his weapon on Tess' body. Liz spun around and fired the flare, center mass, into Vladimir as shots rang out. Crystal jumped up and kicked the gun from Estragon's hand as Weston swung his massive arms and engulfed a startled Estragon, he then lifted him above his head and threw him overboard into the middle of the writhing eels.

Vladimir clutched his smoldering chest, staggered backwards from the impact of the flare and fell overboard. Both sides of the boat irrupted in a frenzy of carnivorous ecstasy. There was a bit of screaming and then silence.

"Holy, moly!!! Are those monsters like the 'Shrieking Eels,' in the movie the Princess Bride?" Missy was peering over the side. "Because I gotta tell y'all that was one nasty way to go, even for those fellas."

Crystal bent over, helped Deb to her feet and then laughingly embraced Missy. "Missy, you are priceless; you have to join the Sisterhood; I'll even train you myself."

"You're on! I haven't had this much fun and excitement since my bronco riding days. Did I ever tell you about the time

. . . ?" Missy and Crystal helped Deb into the bow of the boat, set her down and began to work on her ankle.

Meanwhile, Weston and Liz were greeting the six (three men and three women) operatives that were boarding the boat. The agents seemed stunned by the nature of the attack and the efficient way everyone on board had handled the two intruders. Of course, they knew better than to ask whom these people really were. Their job was to secure the occupants of the boat and retrieve the Flame.

"Ladies and gentlemen, we were sent by President Thomson to protect you. I apologize for the abysmal job that we have done so far. Don't worry, we have your backs now. We will go with you to shore and work out the details from there. I need to get the president on the horn because she wants to speak with Jack. Sir, are you okay?" The Seal Team Six member rushed to Jack's side as everyone turned to look in horror at a devastating tableau.

Liz screamed and ran to Jack as the others crowded around the stern. Jack was covered in blood cradling Tess in his arms. Tess was on her stomach, unresponsive.

"Sir, let Katie look at her." The team leader moved out of the way as a female agent expertly knelt down and began to roll Tess over. Jack gently assisted as Tess was moved on her back in his arms. There was a collective intake of breath.

Tess' eyes were closed and her face was covered in blood. As Katie gently slid the zipper down on Tess' wet suit more blood poured from her chest.

"Oh, God in heaven!!! No, no, no!!!" Jack began to rock Tess' lifeless body back and forth.

CHAPTER TWENTY-SEVEN

Jack stood looking out of the green curtained windows. The bright summer sunlight backlit the cheerful prints hanging on the pale yellow walls. "If you don't stop giving me grief I'm going to leave you here in the hospital and go back to Wyoming for Christmas by myself. Thor will at least be happy to see me."

Tess plumped up the stark white pillows of her hospital bed and snuggled down into the sheets. "I'm just repeating what Missy told me. She said, and I quote, 'Then he cried out to God like a prophet of old to bring you back to him,' that's more or less the gist of it."

"It's not funny. How were we to know that you were covered in Deb's blood from her ankle wound, it looked pretty grisly and you were unconscious. You did end up with a concussion from being shoved aside and hitting your head on the ladder." Jack walked over and sat on Tess' bed; slowly he began to run his fingers through her hair making sure to avoid the bandaged section of her forehead.

"Let's remember that I have not brought up the fact that you threatened to kill them, eat them and make their skins into a coat. I can just imagine you traipsing about in a human skin coat. You are one scary woman, my beloved." Jack smiled.

"Look, I didn't say anything about eating them. Vladimir said that. I was just trying to throw them off-guard by talkin' crazy until everyone could get into place. Oh, yeah, I was such a help there at the end. What with the brilliant move of getting knocked out; it was all part of my master plan." Tess reached up and pulled Jack close for a long, lingering kiss.

"Now, when can we go home? I need about a month of snow, roaring fires and hot cocoa before I head back to work. Or should I say, we head back to work. Jack, I'm so happy that we will be together at the university. I can't wait for you to meet my friends Patty and Tristan." She snuggled against him.

"The doc said a couple more days, just to watch the concussion and then we can fly home. Deb, Nana and Papa will go back with us. Crystal checked on you late last night and then she headed off to D.C. for Christmas with her family. Weston, Leigh-Anne and Missy spoke with the doc and then went back to Wollstonecraft House to give Alex and Theo the news. Deb, Liz, Nana and Papa have not left, can I let them in?" Jack looked anxiously at Tess.

"Sure, I feel fine. Teasing you always puts me in a good mood." Tess was grinning when Jack let the rest of the gang in.

"Oh, honey, you had us so worried." Nana rushed to Tess' side as Papa joined her.

"I know you are tough as granite, but don't do that again." Papa leaned over and gently kissed her forehead.

"I don't try to worry you two; it just keeps happening." Tess held tightly onto both of her grandparents' hands. "Hey, Jack, I forgot to ask. What happened to your nose? It's all bandaged up." Tess looked from one to the other as the room fell silent. "What? What's going on? What are you not telling me?"

"Oh, look at the time!" Liz turned on the television as everyone grabbed chairs and arranged themselves in a semi-circle by Tess' bed. "Look we can talk about Jack's nose later. Right now they are showing President Thomson giving the Flame, the Blood, whatever the blasted thing is called, back to the Indian government."

CNN broke into their regularly scheduled program to show the ceremony. President Thomson, standing in the Oval Office looking regal in a purple suit, was holding the Flame in her hands. She said a few ceremonial words about the friendship between India and the United States while she handed the Indian ambassador the Flame.

Reporters fired away with questions regarding the discovery, which President Thomson handled with her usual aplomb. The official story was that the Flame, or Blood as it was being referred to in the media, had been discovered in a cave in California by amateur archeologists, who had contacted the local university. The university had then reached out to the federal government.

The Indian ambassador was holding the Flame as he gratefully thanked the people of the United States and explained that India would be presenting the discoverers with a substantial reward.

"What the heck! I know that woman." Tess was pointing to a statuesque brunette standing slightly behind the ambassador.

"I think the commentator said she was the ambassador's daughter. How would you know her?" Deb looked over at Tess.

"Well, I guess I can share all of my secrets with you guys. She kidnapped me after I escaped from Jack." Tess put up her hands as everyone tried to talk at once. "Wait, wait, it's a long story. Let's just say, 'no harm, no foul,' and leave it for now. Hi, doc what's the good word?" Tess greeted the doctor as she opened the door.

"Well, Ms. Rankin, I'd say you are going to be right as rain." The doctor leaned over and looked into Tess' eyes with a penlight. "Please follow the light." Tess did as she was told. She preformed various tasks as the doctor checked for any lingering signs of concussion. Tess' head was sore but her intellectual capabilities were fine. She was happy to comply with the checkup.

"We have an eight day concussion protocol, however, you needn't spend it all in hospital. You can go home today, provided that you agree to rest and check in with me before you fly home. Oh, and just to reassure you about the baby, I brought several pictures from the ultrasound. The diving and the accident have not hurt the baby in any way." With a kindly look, the doctor handed Tess' several pictures, nodded to the people in the room and left.

A bewildered Tess looked at the pictures in her hand. A stunned silence descended upon the group. This was not the way they had discussed breaking the news to Tess. Slowly, as if approaching a wildly unpredictable predator, Jack moved toward Tess' bed.

Tess uttered one word. "Jack."

"Baby, before you rip my head off let me explain. I fell in love with you watching you all that time. I mean I was crazy about you and not really thinking straight. I thought if I could just get you to connect with me somehow, maybe you would fall for me too." Jack tried to touch Tess' arm; she pulled away.

"So you thought what, 'I'll get her pregnant and then she'll have to marry me,' of all the irresponsible, stupid, arrogant . . ." Tess seemed to run out of steam.

"I know, I know, I'm so, so sorry. I poked holes in the condoms and orchestrated the kidnapping to coincide with when you were ovulating. I'm an ass! You can make me pay the rest of our lives. Look Papa already broke my nose if that helps." Jack tried his patented grin.

Tess looked down at the pictures in her hands. She shuffled them back and forth as she slowly scanned every inch. "Thanks Papa, he deserved it. Jack, you are wrong about this. I have choices. This is the twenty-first century."

Missy moved a bit forward. "Look Tess, there is no excuse for what Jack did; it was reprehensible. Please don't take it out on the baby. I'll I'm sayin' is that a baby is a gift from God." Missy burst into tears and ran from the room.

"Oh for crying out loud!!" Tess looked at the softly closing door. "Nana and Papa would you please tell Missy that of course I'm keeping the baby; I'm just not sure if I'm keeping Jack." Nana and Papa walked to the bed in unison, kissed each of Tess' cheeks and silently filed out the door.

Jack went back to the windows as Deb and Liz sat on either side of Tess. "Let's see the pictures, you can't really tell anything. It kinda looks like a big kidney bean. So I guess this means that next summer we won't be going on a mission." Liz jokingly nudged Tess.

"Well, all I know is that now I have to go home and have lots of sex with my husband. Of course it's a mighty burden, but I'm willing to make the sacrifice. I won't let you down Tess. I will keep our pact that we made in grade school to have babies at the same time and raise them together. Edward will be thrilled; he's been bugging me for years about getting pregnant." Deb laughingly hugged Tess.

As tears began to stream down Tess' face, Liz gathered her in her arms. "Awe, sweetie, don't cry. We won't leave you. We will all be there every step of the way; you won't be alone. Auntie Liz and Auntie Deb will help with everything. Just think, Nana and Papa are going to be great grandparents. Gregg's wife will be your doctor and watch you like a hawk. Honey, we are a village and we will raise the baby together."

"Thanks." Tess managed to gulp out.

Liz stood up as Deb hugged Tess. "Tess, I know this was not the right way to do it, but please don't cut Jack out of your life." Deb looked at Jack, who put his non-injured hand over his face as he began to cry. "He's an idiot, but he loves you and he's the baby's father." Deb rose from the bed and walked out the door with Liz.

Tess looked at Jack's shaking shoulders. He reached over, grabbed several tissues off the nightstand and moped up his face. Then he turned to her and handed her the rest. "Sorry." Was the only word he could manage.

Then Tess knew. She just knew. It was all before her. Not like her life flashing before her eyes. More of an unshakable knowledge of where she was going and what she was meant to do. Deb was right, Jack was an idiot, but dammit, he was her idiot. He had gone about his courtship in the most wrong-headed, and let's face it, weird way possible, but he had risked his life for her and she loved him.

"If I was feeling better I'd knock the wind out of you; then you would know how I feel." Tess looked up at Jack.

"I'm sorry. I will keep saying 'I'm sorry,' until you believe me. Let's table the physical battery for now, with the broken nose and the cast, I don't think I'm up to it. If you want to have at me when I have healed that's fine, just not the man-parts, I'm going to need those." Jack broke into a broad grin as Tess began to laugh.

"Jack, I don't even know where to begin with you. What you did was so wrong, so careless and so creepy. Honestly, what kind of a maniac plans something like that."

"I know, right! What the hell was I thinking??? I promise to work on the wrongheadedness, carelessness and especially the creepy aspects of my behavior. So what say you my lady? I promise to be a good boy from now until the end of the world. Unless of course you want me to be a bad boy, then I'll dress up." Jack relaxed visibly as Tess barked out another laugh.

Tess held out her hand as Jack enveloped her in his arms. He stretched out on the bed beside her and breathed a sigh of relief.

"So you know the baby is a girl, because that's the kind of luck we have." Tess spoke into Jack's chest.

"I know, I have already begun to call her Sara in my thoughts." Jack squeezed Tess tightly.

"What if it's a boy? Then how will Sara equate to a boy's name?" Tess enquired.

"If it's a boy we will just call him Butch, it's simpler that way." Jack laughed.

"I assume that the plan now is to spoil me into submission until I agree to marry you." Tess looked up at Jack.

"Well, you have cracked my evil plot Miss Marple. Seriously, though, I have invited all of our friends and family to the Double R for New Year's Eve just in case you might want to ring in the New Year by getting married. No pressure."

"It sounds as if you were pretty sure of yourself."

"No, not sure of myself, sure of you."

"Jack."

"You don't even need to say it. I'm running out the door to Fergburger right now."

CHAPTER TWENTY-EIGHT

"So did it hurt like hell? I've heard that natural childbirth can be wicked painful." Liz handed Tess a glass of lemonade as she dropped down on the porch swing next to her.

"Compared to other things that have happened to me, it was dead easy. The best part is when they hand you the baby. Sara was so cute and slimy and pink. Boy was she screaming. I thought Jack was going to pass-out, what a wuss." Tess laughed as Deb pulled up a chair and joined them.

"Let's not get graphic. I still have two months to go. I want to remain in blissful ignorance a bit longer." Deb patted her big belly. "On a serious note, Miz Robinson and Jack's mom want to speak with us. Are you up for it?" Deb did a waving motion as Tess nodded. Miz Robinson, Nana and Nancy walked out the front door and pulled two more chairs toward the women to form a circle.

The six women sat quietly on the front porch gratefully basking in the warm rays of an other-worldly beautiful summer day. The only sound for miles was the continual hum of bees feasting on the flowers in the semi-circular beds that surrounded the porch. Tess assumed that this was Sisterhood business, however, if that were the case then why was Miz Robinson present.

"Ladies, we need to fill you in on a few details regarding your last operation. I wanted to wait until Tess had the baby and things calmed down a bit. Tess, you and Liz don't know that Miz Robinson is a member of the Sisterhood. Deb has been informed but we asked her to keep it quiet for a while. I'll let Miz Robinson explain." Nancy sat back in her chair and began to drink her lemonade.

"Well, my babies, it's like this. I was a sharpshooter in the Army when I met Edward's daddy. My, but he was handsome, in a bad boy sort of way, if y'all know what I mean." She paused as the women nodded their heads in understanding.

"I fell for that man like a boulder off a cliff. The beatings didn't start until we were married and had Edward. At first it was just when he was drinkin', then it got real bad. I resolved to take Edward and leave him, but I knew with his military training and family connections he would hunt me down like a bloodhound." Miz Robinson passed her hand over her eyes as if trying to dispel ghosts from the past.

"One night he came home and tried to strangle me. I grabbed my gun from under the sofa and shot him. Even with his family being powerful in all, no charges were ever brought against me. It was ruled 'self-defense,' and I grabbed Edward and high-tailed it out of the county. I was working in a diner in Memphis when a woman asked to speak with me after work. I agreed and it turned out that she was from the Sisterhood. She had recognized me from the papers." She took a long drink from her lemonade.

"The woman knew of my military background and she figured I would be the perfect Guardian Angel for Tess. She said that Tess needed someone fierce to protect her and I jumped at the chance. Y'all know the rest of the story." Miz Robinson looked to Nancy.

"So, there you have it. The Sisterhood has a special Guardian Angel unit that is tasked with protecting the Keepers." Nancy raised her hand up to stop Tess' objections. "We will not negotiate regarding this extra level of protection. Deb had to be told, so we are now looping you in."

Tess looked from Nancy to Miz Robinson. This latest revelation finally fit in the last piece of the puzzle regarding the Flame. "Are you the one who 'disappeared,' Malcolm?"

"It's more complicated than that Baby Doll. I didn't kill Malcolm. I got him out and turned him over to Nancy, who handed him off to several federal agents; apparently he was wanted by the FBI." Miz Robinson locked eyes with Tess.

"So what about Nathan? You just told us you were an Army sharpshooter. That was an extraordinarily precise shot." Tess reached for the ice-cold lemonade container and poured more golden liquid into Miz Robinson's glass.

"Wait, before anyone says another word, I need you three women to promise that this conversation ends here. We will never speak of this again." Nancy looked on as Liz, Deb and Tess nodded in agreement. "Okay, you can proceed."

"When the alert came that you had been taken I was the only agent close enough to act. I followed your tracking device and waited outside the Old Miller Place. I'm ashamed to say that I didn't get the mobile listening device up quickly enough to hear you being water-boarded." Tess leaned over and patted Miz Robinson's wringing hands.

"Anyway, I listened and waited and listened and waited. It seemed as if you had decided to let the interrogation go on until you could find out the info they had on the Sisterhood. Eventually your extraction team showed up, but I was the only one with the ability to preform a long distance Final Solution. I set up and took the shot upon your signal. I'm not sorry and I would do it again. I am your Guardian Angel and that is what I am tasked to do. Now, me and my Gentleman Caller, are off to church to atone for our sins." Miz Robinson stood up, kissed Tess on the forehead and went inside to collect Sheriff Mike.

"So, that happened." Liz looked around the women at the porch.

"Yep, who would have guessed that my mother-in-law was such a badass. If the men in our lives really knew the true story about us, they'd never get a wink of sleep." Deb laughed as the others joined in.

"Wow, I'm not sure whether to be impressed or terrified. I suppose I'm a bit of both. Nancy, since I'm a mom and I have your unpredictable son as my husband, I will agree to the Guardian Angel protection. Now what's up with the Sisterhood?" Tess enquired.

"Obviously, you do not have an assignment this summer. Liz and Crystal will be leaving for 'parts unknown,' next week. Missy has joined us and she is spending this summer training with Niels. After Deb has recovered from her pregnancy we would like to train her to be an operative just in case ghosts from our past come to Jameson." Nancy paused as Deb gave the thumbs up signal.

"Please tell us we won't have any repercussions from last year." Liz looked at Nancy.

"None. President Thomson has taken care of everything; she has some wiz-kid computer genius named Courtney working on removing all electronic traces of the Sisterhood. Between Courtney, Alex and Theo, we are golden. Leigh-Anne and the board have taken care of all the financials, so we are back in business." Nancy paused as a harried looking Jack burst out the door gently cradling a wailing Sara.

"Okay, enough business talk. Sara is really upset. I think you need to feed her." Jack thrust Sara into Tess' arms. Tess tucked Sara under her blouse and began to breast feed her.

"I thought she needed to be changed." A very nervous Mason paced the porch. "But Edward was all like, 'No, she needs to be burped,' and I kept reminding him that you don't burp babies that haven't just eaten."

"Your answer to everything is changing a diaper! I'm telling you according to the books gas can be agony." Edward looked to Deb in agreement, as Dave stood by Nancy silently grinning.

"Hey, Three Men and a Baby, calm down. You guys do know that Sara has each and every one of you whipped. It's pathetic, honestly; two deputies and a college professor." Tess laughed as the men attempted to protest.

"They're right. She's trying to tell us something. If you would just read the books I bought you then we could all be on board with Team Sara." Jack hovered around his wife and baby.

"Jack." Tess leveled a look at her husband.

"I'm only saying that Sara is an unusually expressive child and, according to my research, she will need a very special environment to grow and flourish." Jack patted Sara's head under Tess' shirt.

"Jack, she's five weeks old." Tess looked up at her clearly smitten husband.

"It's never too early. I loaded dozens of articles on your laptop that I think you should read." Jack continued on as Tess regarded him with lovingly amused eyes.

MY AMAZING INTERNS

ABOUT THE AUTHOR

Ali Roberti is a history professor in California, who has traveled extensively throughout the world. While working for the University of Maryland, Ali lived in Cairo, Lisbon and London. These life experiences provide the rich backdrop and authentic voice for her novels. Ali married her college sweetheart and they now live on a ranch in Northern California with their three children.

CPSIA information can be obtained
at www.ICGtesting.com
Printed in the USA
LVHW012039080120
642937LV00014B/856/P